Milton Hicks was a real warrior of old Texas, a Cherokee breed who had fought with Andy Jackson in Louisiana against the Red Sticks. He came to Texas and continued to follow the path of the gun. Not much is known about him, other than that he was a brave man and a resourceful fighter. He never owned land, voted, married, or joined the Catholic Church (which was necessary for citizenship in this state of old Mexico). He died in a battle with the Comanche.

Now this hero of the Old West is brought to searing life by his descendant, Captain D. L. "Pappy" Hicks, a modern-day hero who fought in Korea and Vietnam, who led the Montagnards of the Central Highlands against the Viet Cong, and was famed as a master of the Gurkha kukri knife—"The Great Silencer."

Only a historian, a guerrilla fighter, and a master storyteller could have brought Milton Hicks to epic life.

QUANTITY SALES

Most Dell books are available at special quantity discounts when purchased in bulk by corporations, organizations, and special-interest groups. Custom imprinting or excerpting can also be done to fit special needs. For details write: Dell Publishing, 666 Fifth Avenue, New York, NY 10103. Attn.: Special Sales Department.

INDIVIDUAL SALES

Are there any Dell books you want but cannot find in your local stores? If so, you can order them directly from us. You can get any Dell book in print. Simply include the book's title, author, and ISBN number if you have it, along with a check or money order (no cash can be accepted) for the full retail price plus $1.50 to cover shipping and handling. Mail to: Dell Readers Service, P.O. Box 5057, Des Plaines, IL 60017.

BREED'S RAMPAGE

Captain D. L. "Pappy" Hicks

A DELL BOOK

Published by
Dell Publishing
a division of
The Bantam Doubleday Dell
Publishing Group, Inc.
1 Dag Hammarskjold Plaza
New York, New York 10017

Dell ® TM 681510, Dell Publishing,
a division of the Bantam Doubleday Dell Publishing Group, Inc.

ISBN: 0-440-20020-2

Printed in the United States of America
Published simultaneously in Canada

July 1988

10 9 8 7 6 5 4 3 2 1

OPM

MILTON HICKS:
A Character Sketch

Milton Hicks is a dark and little known figure in Texas history.

Milton was born about 1798 in the Cherokee Nation, which is now Tennessee. He was the grandson of Chief Charles Hicks, Principal Chief of the Cherokee Nation who died in 1827.

When the Cherokee joined Jackson's Army to fight against the Red Sticks of the Creek Indian Nation in the War of 1812, Milton, who was then about sixteen, went along as a young warrior. After the Red Sticks had been vanquished, most of the Cherokee went back home. A few others, Milton included, went with Jackson to New Orleans. After the war, Milton came to Texas.

Much of what Milton Hicks did in Texas remains a mystery. There are no records to indicate that he was ever married, owned land, voted, owed debts, held public office, served on a jury, was ever arrested for any crime, or was a convert to Catholicism, which was required by both Spanish and Mexican law to become a citizen of Mexico.

The only documents that mention Milton Hicks list him as a member of some armed force. He fought against Indians with the Spanish, Mexican, and Texas Republic governments. It can be assumed that the gun was his only vocation.

He was a member of the Anglo Settler's army that captured Fort Velasco, June 1832. His leg was shattered in that battle.

In January 1839, he was killed along with fourteen other

men in a group called the "Webster Party." They were ambushed by Comanche Indians on Brushy Creek, just north of present day Austin, Texas. Only their skeletal remains were ever found, identified by Milton Hicks' broken leg.

Historical Characters

Milton Hicks—*Cherokee-Anglo breed*

Peter Ellis Bean—*Anglo, Mexican Indian Agent*

Frost Thorn—*Anglo, merchant in Nacogdoches*

Haden Edwards—Anglo, Nacogdoches, leader of Fredonia Rebellion

Diwali—Cherokee, War Chief of the Cherokees

Big Mush—Cherokee, Peace Chief of the Cherokees

The Egg—Cherokee, war leader

Nicolet—Cherokee, war leader

Adolphus Sterne—German-Jew, Merchant in Nacogdoches

Colonel José de las Piedras—Mexican Army, Commander of East Texas

Long King—Coushatta Indian, War Chief

Vicente Cordova—Mexican, leader in Nacogdoches

James Gaines—Sabine Settlement, Gaines's Ferry at Sabine River

Almanzón Houston—leader in Ayish Bayou

Stephen Prather—Anglo, owner Prather's Indian Trading Post

James B. (Brit) Bailey—Anglo, old settler around Brazoria

Battise—Alabama Indian, son of chief and later chief

William Goyens—mulatto, wealthy businessman in Nacogdoches

Fictional Characters

Francisca Ruis—Mexican at Nacogdoches
Isaac—black slave at Will Goyens' Stable
The Wisp—Ayish Bayou Settlement
Nat Ellis—operator of Gaines's Ferry
Eb—outlaw in Neutral Strip
Reed—outlaw in Neutral Strip
Plunder—outlaw in Neutral Strip
Plug—outlaw in Neutral Strip
Big Red—camp leader in Neutral Strip
Tiny—outlaw in Neutral Strip
Lion Jaw—outlaw in Neutral Strip
Colbert Family, Acadians in Neutral Strip
  Pepin—father
  Mama—mother
  Richard—son
  Philippe Fave—son-in-law
  Maria Fave—daughter of Pepin
  Claudette—daughter of Richard
  Rosemarie—daughter of Pepin
Morning Light—Quapaw Indian woman
Thumping Turtle—Coushatta-Mexican breed, Milton's chase

BREED'S RAMPAGE

Chapter One

The huge man lifted a quart-sized stone jug to his lips and guzzled rum down his gullet. He had drunk so much during the day that the fiery "Indian rum" no longer burned his throat. In fact, at this stage of his drinking, not much bothered him.

The half-breed sat on a fallen tree trunk, doing his best to empty the jug held loosely in a huge paw. Thumping Turtle was large and dark like his mother's people, the Coushatta Indian tribe. He stood six feet three inches tall in his moccasins and weighed two hundred and twenty-five pounds. He showed none of his father's Spanish blood. That was all right with Thumping Turtle. He hated Spanish people, especially the Spanish father he had never seen. Some said his father was a Catholic priest. He did not know, nor did he care.

He sat on a tree trunk on the edge of a small meadow. The breed didn't notice the young deer grazing with no fear, for the fall hunting season was long past, nor the owl hooting a soft song that only a mate of his own species understood. He did not see the great nocturnal bird drop from the limb of its perch in a large pine tree and start tracking a rat by sound as it ran across the small meadow. The owl scooped the rat up in its powerful claws. The rat struggled as the bird flew off in search of its mate.

The man did not see the young deer look up at the sound of the owl's attack, then return to his meal of tender late-spring grass when he saw that he was not in danger.

All of these acts of nature were lost upon this man of the forest. The man's only reason for existence at the moment was to get as drunk as he could. He had been working on it for two days, following Mexican rum dealers as he drank.

Thumping Turtle took another swig from the jug. It was nearly empty. He would have to go see the white men again for more rum. He hated those men, as he did all white men. But he liked their rum.

One more short pull on the jug and it was empty. He struggled to his feet. He needed more rum, and he was going to get more rum. He knew where the Mexicans had camped. If he had not known, he would have been able to find them by their smell. White men seemed never to take a bath.

The breed stumbled across the meadow. The deer jerked its head in the air at the noise and with its tail held high, bounded for the safety of the thick pine forest.

Thumping Turtle walked across the meadow and went crashing through the forest like a wounded bear. This was not a quiet Indian on the hunt. At least not a hunt for wild game. The breed did not stop until he came to the small clearing by the creek where the two whiskey traders were bedded down for the night.

One of the Mexican men woke to find Thumping Turtle standing over him. "What do you want, man?"

"More rum," demanded Thumping Turtle.

"Go away, Turtle. Come in the morning," the Mexican told the breed.

"It is morning now," insisted Turtle.

"Sí, the middle-of-the-night morning," the Mexican grumbled. "You got money, Indian? You got anything to trade?"

"You got my money. You got my horse. You got everything. I have nothing," admitted Turtle. He stood tall, but not very steady.

"Then why would I want to deal with you?" the Mexican demanded in an irritated voice.

"Maybe you trade for my knife," Turtle said hopefully. He took the knife from its sheath. "It is a good knife. Big."

"I have a knife. I don't want another knife," the Mexican

told him, pulling the blanket up over his head. He mumbled, "Bloodthirsty mosquitoes are eating me up."

"Knife for rum," demanded Turtle. Anger stirred in his voice.

"No money, no rum. No good trade, no rum," the Mexican said with a voice of finality.

"Hey, man, let a man sleep," complained the second Mexican from his bedroll.

"It's Turtle. He wants more rum," the first man said.

"Then sell him some and let's get to sleep," said the second man.

"He don't have anything," the first man informed him.

The second Mexican was shorter-tempered than the first. "Look, you drunken Indian, tomorrow we will be at the Coushatta village. Get some of your people to give you trading material. Until then, get out of our camp!"

The two Mexicans rolled and shifted to more comfortable positions.

Thumping Turtle was left standing, looking at the dark forms on the ground. The fire had died to glowing embers and did not light the area. Drunken anger began to rise from the pit of Turtle's gut to his already unsteady head. He wanted rum. He was going to get rum.

His knife was already drawn. These were only white men, of no importance to an Indian. With a wild-sounding roar he jerked the blanket back from the man at his feet and nearly severed his head from his body with the knife.

The second man gave a gasp at the sound of the fierce yell. He was a man of the trail and slept prepared. He cocked and fired the musket he had been sleeping with.

Thumping Turtle's war cry increased in volume as he closed in for the kill. The Mexican tried to kick free from the blanket. He screamed as the blade gutted him.

The horses squealed in sudden fright at the noise and the smell of fresh blood. They settled down after a moment of quiet.

Turtle ignored the slight pain of the wound made by the musketball that had plowed through the flesh of his left arm. He had received worse injuries playing Indian stickball.

He threw more wood on the smoldering fire for better light to help his search for more rum. After a short search he found the pack of rum. With a roar of delight he pulled out the cork of a jug and threw it into the creek.

Rum, and all alcoholic beverages, were, by Mexican law, not to be sold to Indians. These two had paid with their lives for breaking that law.

Turtle was glad when men such as these broke the law. They brought rum and whiskey for him. This time they had given him plenty.

In a short time the breed was dead to the world in a drunken stupor.

It was midmorning before Thumping Turtle struggled to a sitting position. Ants had found his overturned jug and had made trails across his legs and to the entrance of their homes in the ground. He brushed them off and sat moaning, his head held in his hands. His head hurt, his mouth was sticky and needed moisture, his stomach heaved, and he needed another drink.

He found a full gallon jug of rum and used it to lower the noise in his ears and to settle his heaving stomach.

After his medicine-by-jug he looked at his new booty, ignoring the dead Mexicans. He had plenty of everything!

Turtle caught the hobbled horses. He found his own saddle, rifle, pistol, and tomahawk. Now he had his own horse back and two more saddle horses, plus a pack mule. Most important of all, he had rum! Twenty-six gallons of rum! All he needed now was someone to drink with.

Turtle loaded the pack mule and saddled the other two horses. He was not used to robbery on the trail; he didn't bother to search the Mexican for money. He had what he'd come for, rum.

He stepped aboard his horse and rode off, driving the other

animals ahead of him. The two dead Mexicans were left in their bedrolls.

Early that afternoon, Thumping Turtle rode into the small farm of a Mexican settler.

The woman had seen him from a distance, swaying in the saddle with a jug in his hand. She recognized the three animals he drove before him. They belonged to two rumrunners. She knew the Indian, and he was a mean one when drunk. He must have been very mean to get those horses and mule.

She gathered her children to her and ran to the root cellar with them. She sent them inside and urged them to remain quiet no matter what happened. After closing the cloth flap used for a door, she walked to the front of the hut to wait for her drunken visitor. She wished her husband had not gone to help a neighbor.

Thumping Turtle rode to the hut and stopped. The two horses and mule broke through the brush fence and started eating on the new corn in the fields around the hut. The woman wanted to scream and chase the animals out of her fields, but she knew she must act right around this man and not anger him.

Turtle looked at the silent woman before him. "Ah, José Rodríguez's woman! Where is José? Hey, man, come out here. Let's have some rum!"

"José is not here," the woman told him. She had to stand firm and brave. "He will be here any moment."

Turtle looked around the small place. The hut was standard East Texas Mexican settler's style with stakes driven into the ground for walls, and mud packed in the cracks to make it solid. The roof was grass thatched. There were no windows, the front door being the only entrance.

"Ah, José's mule, he is not here!" Turtle exclaimed. He looked at the woman again. "Maybe you drink with Turtle, yes?"

"I am sorry, sir, I do not drink," she informed him, an edge of fear in her voice.

The breed nearly fell on his face as he got off his horse. "I going to teach you to drink, yes?"

She backed from him, nearly falling over a small stool. The wall of the hut stopped her progress. Fear had come to her eyes and her face twisted in dread. She had heard many stories about how Indians would rape a woman, as many as ten or fifteen men enjoying themselves with one woman. Drunk Indians were the worst. They preyed upon helpless women and children. There was no help for her. Not even God would help her.

The big breed staggered toward her.

She fled from him, running around the hut and down the trail in the rear. She had to stay away from this insane man!

Turtle was stopped by the wall also. He looked around, trying to find the woman. Where had she gone? She had run from him and it angered him. He started throwing baskets, bowls, and utensils that were located on a bench in front of the hut. His anger was terrible.

The woman stopped. *My God, what if he finds the children?* flashed through her mind.

She knew she had to distract him so he would not search the place and accidentally stumble on her children. She ran around the hut and stopped. She screamed at him, "Hey, you, stop destroying my things!"

His eyes found her and he staggered toward her. She was not a beauty, but she was a woman and he needed a woman. It made little difference if he could perform a manly act or not, his desire was for a woman, now!

The woman stood her ground until he got close. As he reached for her, she ran through the hole in the fence and started across the cornfield, flapping her arms and screaming at him. She acted like a mother quail leading a hunter from her nest and little ones.

Turtle started after her in a lumbering run that quickly ate up the distance between them. Suddenly he was upon her. He grabbed her and threw her to the ground, falling on top of her. He brutally spread her legs apart.

The woman went into an angry rage, clawing at his face and neck. She bit his arm with the viciousness of a fighting bitch dog.

The breed grabbed her around the neck with both hands and stood straight up, roaring in painful anger. He shook her as if she were a corn-husk doll.

When she became quiet and still in his hands, he looked at her a moment. She was dead! He threw her lifeless form to the ground. "Dumb Mexican bitch. She won't hurt Turtle no more."

The fuss had made him thirsty. He went back to where his horse stood ground-hitched and found the jug broken where he had dropped it.

"Good horse. You stay put where Turtle put," he mumbled to the animal. "All right, horse, we go!"

He climbed into the saddle. All of the rum was on the pack mule. He needed to catch that mule. He kicked his horse into a trot, riding through the hole in the fence and into the corn-field.

The two saddle horses saw him coming. The two horses kicked up their heels and ran off in a southerly direction. They jumped the fence and kept going at a run. They didn't aim to be caught.

The pack mule saw the man on the horse coming for him. The animal broke and ran for the treeline. As it ran into the forest, it kept sideswiping trees as it ran. The mule ran and pitched until a thick clump of brush and limbs of the thicket reached out and grabbed his halter, bringing him to a halt.

Turtle rode up mumbling under his breath on the rough course of action he was going to take toward the mule.

He freed the mule from the thicket and dug into the bags for another jug of rum. All of them were broken and the bags were wet from spilled rum. There was nothing left but shat-tered clay.

He staggered around to the front of the mule for some serious talking. "Hey, you, mule, you spill my rum! You damn Mexican like your owners. This is Thumping Turtle who owns you now. I teach you better."

Turtle drew back a huge fist and hit the mule between the eyes. The mule dropped to his knees as if it had been shot.

The breed looked silently down at the fallen animal. Then it came to him. "Hey, mule, you will be my rum! I sell you for rum. You get me plenty rum. When a man has rum, he has women!"

He jerked hard on the lead rope and the animal staggered to its feet. Turtle laughed. "Now you stagger like me! But I bet you no run from Turtle no more. Next time I eat you."

Turtle rode out of the woods and looked across the field at the settler's hut. He had better ride on away from here before the woman's man came back. White men's laws did not like Indians who killed their women. Spanish law was even stricter than most.

He sat his horse a moment, deciding which way to go. The two saddle horses had gone south. Perhaps he could find them down the trail. But south was also the Mexican town of Liberty. The town was now flooded with Anglo-American settlers. If they found out about the two dead Mexican men and the dead Mexican woman, they would gladly string him up in some oak tree. Not because the white Anglos would care about the white Mexican people, but only because it would be a good excuse to get rid of another red man.

He turned his horse north, in the direction of Nacogdoches. It would take a while before the news of the dead Mexicans reached there. By that time he would have his rum and be gone.

Turtle did not see the four small children run out into the cornfield to find their dead mother. Under other circumstances a feeling of remorse might have come over him. But a drunk Thumping Turtle would have gone back and killed them all.

Chapter Two

A tall, dark man watched the two horses approach. One horse carried Peter Ellis Bean, Indian agent for the District of East Texas. The Mexican government had made him a lieutenant colonel for his services in their fight for independence from Spain. He had served them well then, and he'd continued to serve them.

His young son, Samuel, rode the second horse. The boy's schooling had not been in formal classrooms, but in the rough-and-tumble life on the Mexican frontier. At his young age he was fluent in English, Spanish, and a half-dozen Indian languages. There were very few experienced hunters who could track and read sign as well as this young boy.

The tall man turned toward the log house and said something into the opening used for a door. He spoke in the language of the Ani-Tsalagi American Indian.

A tall elderly man stepped from the small house and awaited the arrival of the two riders. There was a bearing of confident dignity in this man of mature years. He was the principal chief and the war chief of the Texas Cherokees, called Diwali, "Bowl." He was better known to the whites as Chief Bowles. For his part in the Fredonian Rebellion he had been made a lieutenant colonel by the Mexican government.

Whatever he was called by his fellow man, he displayed a physical appearance of power and intelligence.

"Ah, my friend, Tuya, the Bean. Welcome to the home of your friend, Diwali," the chief greeted.

"It is good to be with my old friend again," Bean replied, using fair Tsalagi.

Many of the younger men of the tribe had learned to speak either Spanish or English, or both. The old chief refused to learn either one. Many believed him to be a breed, but no matter what blood flowed through his veins he was Tsalagi through and through.

"And your son. Both of you are welcome. Do you want to eat?" Diwali asked.

"I would be pleased," said Bean.

It was a custom among most American Indian tribes to greet a new arrival with an offer of food. Who knew how long the traveler had been without a meal, it did not matter whether the greeted visitor was a member of the family, a friend, or a complete stranger, the offer was extended to all.

"Milton," Pete greeted the tall man, who sat quietly, out of the picture.

"Pete," Milton returned, no expression on his clean-shaven face. Pale-blue eyes held a curious interest, but otherwise they were vacant of all emotion.

Three other men joined them, Big Mush, who was the peace chief, the Egg, and Nicolet. The three men greeted their friend with pleasure, mixed with respect.

Diwali returned with two bowls of corn gruel and offered them to the two new arrivals.

"How is it with the white men in Nacogdoches?" asked Diwali.

"Growing in numbers," replied Pete.

"Anglos or Mexicans?" Diwali wanted to know.

"Anglos."

"That is bad for Mexico. Worse for Texas," Diwali reflected.

All of the men set in silence while the two finished eating.

A woman stoked a fire and set a pot over the flames. Soon the aroma of an herbal drink could be smelled. The Cherokees had not completely accepted the custom of drinking coffee. There was a belief among many that it was poisonous and would make you die a slow death. The Cherokees of Texas were among the wealthiest people in the area and could afford the expensive imported brew better than anyone else.

When Pete and his son finished eating, the woman brought the hot brew to them. After serving the men, she retreated, leaving the men to talk man talk. She did not leave in obedience to the men in the manner of a white woman or a Comanche woman. This woman was a Cherokee, a Tsagali, and this was her home and her yard, not her husband's. The woman owned all the property, as was the custom of the Ani-Tsalagi.

"Is Piedras still jumping up and down on one leg like a little boy who must pee and is told to wait?" asked Diwali.

All the men laughed.

Pete laughed with them. "Yes. He still feels there is a conspiracy between the U.S. of the North and the Anglo settlers here to take Texas from Mexico."

"Is this the true feeling of the Anglos of the Republic of the North?" Diwali inquired.

"The Anglos of the North always want land," Pete informed him and the others. "They will be satisfied when they set foot in the Pacific Ocean."

"It must be their nature just to want land. All land that is not theirs. Then when they get the land, they fight among themselves over it and won't let those in need use it. Your people are strange indeed," sighed the old chief.

"Aye," agreed Pete.

"What of the Anglo settlers here in Texas?" asked Diwali. "Do they wish to make war on the Mexicans and make Texas American?"

The others nodded their heads, wanting to know what this man who lived with and talked to the Anglos thought. This was an important question to them all.

"Not these white men. They're happy here in Mexico. They are making more money than they could make in America. That is the reason they are here in the first place. And they do not have as much trouble out of the Mexican government as businessmen in America do out of their government," Pete told them.

"That is not what they say. I hear their complaints all the time. Every time I go to Nacogdoches, I hear them wail and cry," said Nicolet, entering the conversation for the first time.

"That's for consumption in Mexico City," Pete told him. "I don't think the white men want to cause Mexico trouble. But you can never tell about the white man. There are many rumors that President Jackson is making secret plans to take Texas away from Mexico."

"That Jackson!" spat Diwali.

"He is a bad man," agreed Chief Big Mush.

"He lies to the red man. A man who lies cannot be trusted," was the observation of Diwali. "He became chief of his people because he tells them that he will drive all the red men west of the Mississippi. Some of those same people protected his head from the Red Sticks' tomahawk at Horseshoe Bend."

"Well, ole Piedras is up in the air about them rumors. He don't trust Anglos here or in the North. You know he's been as nervous as a skunk in a rattlesnake den ever since that Fredonia thing," replied Pete.

"A nervous skunk can get messy," agreed Egg.

"Yes, he is a nervous little man. He should not be. We Ani-Tsalagi and our other Indian allies are here to protect his head against the Anglo settlers and his borders against the Republic of the North," Diwali told Pete.

Pete was white himself, but he knew the old war chief was talking about United States whites. Pete was accepted as a Mexican white, even though his family was English and he had been born in Tennessee. He had been many years in Mexico.

"What of my friends Frost Thorn, Will Goyens, Dolf Sterne, Chireno, and others who treat the Cherokee so well?" asked Diwali.

"They are well. Working to make more money," Pete told him.

"Ah! I do not know about my white friends. They are all the same in that manner. They do not stop and let others gain a good living. They must have it all. Then they do not help others of their own who are not as fortunate as they. They are my friends, but it does me sad to see my friends carry on in such a manner," complained Diwali.

"It is the nature of the white man," Pete told them.

The men shook their heads sadly.

"The Indian leader has less than anyone. He gives all to his people. He keeps just enough to keep him living and not just existing," Diwali told Pete. "His wealth is his honor and the power that his people give him. For a white man to be powerful, it is not what people give him that makes his power. It is how much he can take from his own people. The white people respect only those who can take from them. It is strange."

Pete shrugged.

"Do you come to see me on a matter of importance, or do we dance and enjoy our friendship?" the old chief asked.

"It is always a pleasure to see you. You are an old and true friend. But I came on this trip to see that tall man over there, Milton Hicks," Pete told Diwali.

"Ah," said the chief.

"I wish for him to do something for me. It is for the government," said Pete. "It will take only a few days of his time."

The expression on Hicks' face did not change.

"He can go. There is nothing or no one here to hold him," said Diwali. Then his face cracked and he broke into loud laughter. "He has no home to go to. Two days ago his woman kicked him out of her house. I have given the poor little warrior meals from my own fire."

Diwali laughed heartily. The other three Indian leaders joined him, slapping the ground with their hands in their merriment. Pete could not help but smile, but he did not make a display of his humor.

Milton changed expression for the first time. He grinned.

"Aye, that is true," was his only comment.

Only an American Indian could laugh at Milton Hicks in fun and not have to worry about retribution. It was the custom of the red man to laugh at his fellow man in all things. The red man will laugh at another's discomfort because he is happy that it is not he, and his laughter reminds others that they are after all mere men. But too much laughter could set the breed off on a rampage that could only end in death.

"Tell me what you want," Milton told Pete in flawless English.

"I will go and tend to my business while you tend to yours," said Diwali.

"We must all do the same thing," Big Mush told them.

The four Cherokee leaders excused themselves.

"I have a problem. Do you know Thumping Turtle?" asked Pete.

"The breed Coushatta who considers himself to be a greater warrior than he is?" asked Milton in a matter-of-fact tone.

"Yep, he be the one. But you gotta admit, he's one hell of a warrior."

"Well, he got drunk on some good Anglo rum and went on a rampage. He killed the men who were swilling him. Then he killed a Mexican woman at an isolated farm," Pete told him. "The white men were from the Liberty and Anahuac area. The alcalde in Liberty is demanding justice."

"Justice has been served. The two rum sellers were killed," Milton said.

"Can't argue that point. But it's more of a crime to kill a rum peddler than the peddler to sell rum to Indians," Pete informed Milton.

"Rum kills people," Milton said simply.

"True. And most of them rum peddlers needs killing," Pete agreed. "But the laws are laws. Even if you don't agree with them."

"Humph!" Milton had been born and brought up in the Cherokee Nation when clan laws prevailed. If a man was not willing to pay the price for breaking the law, then he did not break it. It was as simple as that. In the blood laws of the clans, breaking most clan laws carried a penalty of death.

"Will you go after him for me? I hear he's bouncing around over in No Man's Land near the border. Some believe the Neutral Strip is still in effect. They think neither Mexican law or American law will cross into the zone. Most won't. But now the border has been settled, more or less, and it's American territory," Pete told Milton. "I need you. Will you go?"

Milton sat, his deadpan look giving no indication of what he was thinking. If he went, Thumping Turtle would either be brought back or left dead upon the field. Not because Thumping Turtle had killed his fellow man. Only because Milton had been asked to go for him by a friend. He was sure that he would have to leave Thumping Turtle upon the field of battle. He was sure that the Coushatta breed would not come back to face white man's justice.

Suddenly his stern look was crinkled by a smile. "The old Bowl said it. I don't have a woman to hold me. I will go."

"As is the case most of the time, I have no money to pay you in cash. But when you go to Nacogdoches, go to Frost Thorn's or Dolf Stern's to get what you need on the trail," Pete told him.

"I go to Thorn's."

"Okay. I wanted you to go after Thumping Turtle for a couple of reasons, Milton. You know him by sight, for one. And I reckon you're one of the few who can take him. Give it a try. But don't git yourself killed. You got a lot more to do for Texas," Pete told him. "And if the American law gives you any trouble, tell them to git in contact with me."

"Maybe it be him to get killed. I won't get," Milton said in his matter-of-fact voice.

Without another word he got up and started getting ready to leave.

That was the signal for Diwali and the other three to return. They continued their visit with Pete. The old chief told Pete that they would have a good dance tonight. He loved to dance and eat. He was also not too old for women.

Pete figured that when he got to be seventy-three years old, he might have to slow down on the woman part.

"Oh, Tladatsi!" Diwali called, using Milton's Cherokee name of Panther Killer, "come back again and we will look for you another woman!"

The men laughed with delight.

Milton rode out of the Diwali's camp with a wave of his hand.

The breed Cherokee carried all that he owned on the back of his horse. He was typical American Indian when it came to believing that the worth of a man was not what he had, but what he did as a man and what he did for others. If a man held many things of value to himself, then he was not a wealthy man or a good man. He was just a greedy man.

He pointed his pony south. Fifty miles of heavy timbered forests, muddy trails, and rain-swollen rivers and creeks stood between him and Nacogdoches.

It was a beautiful early spring day of 1829. Even though it was late in the afternoon, Milton figured a late start was as good as an early one. A man of decision and purpose did not worry about time.

Chapter Three

The hand cart was stuck in knee-deep mud in the middle of the trail. Three children perched on the top of the few belongings the family had loaded in the cart. A worn old pack horse with another load stood to the side of the trail, patiently waiting for his next command.

A man and woman stood dejectedly on each side of the trail, frustrated anger on the man's face. The woman, as worn looking as the horse, stood in abject helplessness.

Milton stopped his horse.

"Mister, if you want to rob me, I ain't got nothing worth stealing. If you wanta give me a hand, I sure could use it," the man said. There was no hope in his voice.

Milton kicked his horse up to the hand cart. "You younguns climb over on my horse."

The oldest boy, about eight, and the oldest girl, nine, slipped in behind Milton. The youngest girl, about five years old, hesitated.

"Jump, honey! He's gonna help us," the father called to the girl.

"God, and we need all the help we can get," sobbed the woman.

Milton smiled at the girl, breaking the solemn look of his face. The little girl held out a hand and stepped to Milton's saddle, trying to ignore the intimidating, rollbacked-eyed look of the horse.

With his extra load, the horse carried his passenger onto firm ground on the side of the trail. Milton let the children to the ground.

"Hold it here while I go up ahead. I'll look for a camp spot," Milton told the man. He kicked his horse down the muddy trail.

"Don't worry, we ain't got no choice but to hold," the man said in a weary voice.

"You ain't gonna leave us, are you, mister?" the woman begged. She was near to tears again.

"No, ma'am, I'll be right back, directly," Milton assured her. He told the man, "Tie a rope to the cart while I'm gone so I can pull it."

He rode a short distance down the trip and found a small clearing just off the trail. He went back to the stranded family.

The man stood in the trail beside the tongue of the cart. A rope had been secured to the cross bar of the cart handles. He was muddy from head to toe. He had had a struggle with the cart. He had tied the horse to the back of the tailgate.

Milton tied the rope to the large, wooden horn of his Mexican saddle and kicked his horse. The horse humped his back under the extra load. He was a war horse, not a draft animal. He backed his ears, bared his teeth, and rolled his eyes.

"Horse, I'm gonna kick hell outta you it you don't settle down." The tone of Milton's voice convinced the horse that his master was not going to take any foolishness from him. When Milton kicked the horse the second time, it moved, pulling the cart along in the deep mud. The man held the tongue of the cart up so it would not drag the ground.

The woman gathered the children and they followed, walking on the firm surface beside the trail.

Milton pulled the cart into the clearing and untied the rope from the saddle horn. He told the man, "If I was you, I think I'd set up here till it dried before I'd move on. Then I'd move between rain spells."

"Thank you for getting us outta that bog," the exhausted man said. "If'n you will, we could give you some coffee if'n we can git a fire started. We only used the grounds three or four times."

"I got a way to go," Milton told him.

"We do too. I'm gettin' out of this here damned place. I'm headin' back to America," the man told Milton.

"Oh, God, we've lost everything here. Everything!" the woman sobbed. "I lost two of my babies. My little babies are gone!"

"All right, Martha, it's gonna be all right," the man comforted her.

The three children huddled around her.

Milton stepped down from his horse. "Are you gonna make it?" It was hard to ask a man that in front of his family.

"We'll make out," the man told him.

"You got food?" Milton asked. Then he added, "For the kids?"

"We ain't got much left," the man admitted.

"Oh, Jacob, we ain't got nothin', nothin' at all! It's gonna be a hungry night again!" the woman sobbed.

This was not the standard strong, resilient frontier woman. She didn't belong here.

Without hesitation Milton stepped to his horse and unstrapped his bedroll. He handed the man some cooked meat that was wrapped in doeskin and a small bag of salt. Then he handed the man a leather pouch.

"This is called *gahawesita* by the Cherokees. It is corn that has been soaked, parched, and pounded into a meal. This is the only food a warrior carries with him on the warpath. It won't make you fat, but it will sustain you. Just add water and drink it."

"Thank you. Tomorrow I'll hunt. We'll make it now," replied the man.

"I'd hunt me an opossum in the moonlight tonight," Milton advised.

"What'll we do for wood?" the woman asked, still ready to burst forth with more sobbing.

"Ma'am, I'd take some of that furniture outta that cart an' use it for firewood," Milton informed her.

"But it's all I've got. I've lost all my furniture as it is," the woman complained.

"That can be replaced," he told her. After a pause for emphasis he added bluntly, "But them kids can't."

"Yes, yes, of course, you're right," the man said. "We'll take all the furniture out we don't need. Then we'll put dried wood in when it dries out to carry in its place."

"Good thinking," said Milton.

Milton handed the woman another small leather sack. "I have some fresh coffee grounds here. Let's make that fire."

Milton and Jacob unloaded the furniture. The tall man took a small amount of powder from his horn and made a small mound at the base of the wood and some splinters for starter wood. He touched the hammer to the flint of his pistol and the powder started burning. In a short while the wood was blazing.

He helped them build a lean-to that would keep them out of the weather. Then he searched for the proper wood for them to lay out in the sun to dry. When he had done all he could, he got on his horse, turned it south, and kicked him out on the trail. He winked at the little girl as he passed. He had to admit that if it hadn't been for the children, he would have left the two adults to themselves.

"Hey, thank you," Jacob called.

"He ain't real friendly, is he?" asked the woman.

"Good God A 'mighty damn!" he said to her, incredulous. He shook his head in wonder.

These were not the first people to come to Texas and find that they could not make it. Whites had been running back and forth over the land ever since Robert de La Salle, the French explorer, passed through in 1684. He had remained in the ancient Indian town of Nacogdoches. He had been well received and aided by the Hasinai Indians during his sickness. When he departed Nacogdoches, he left behind a couple of things the Indians didn't need, white man's diseases and a few men who had deserted his command. The Indians had no immunity to "Old World" diseases, and the coming of La Salle and those diseases signaled the decline of the once powerful Caddo Confederation. More Indians were killed in the New World by white man's diseases than by his gun or his military genius.

With the clearing of the Indians in Texas "by the hand of God," the first white settlement in East Texas was made around 1716 by Father Margil. He founded the mission Our Lady of the Guadalupe of Nacogdoches. Another mission was established just west of Nacogdoches among the Ayish Indians. The good priests started the process of saving their souls, but the good men who saved souls in the name of Jesus Christ caused the extinction of a race of people from the face of the earth.

Because of the push-and-pull efforts of the French and Spanish to control East Texas, most of the population finally cleared the area. The missions went into ruin and disappeared.

Finally some semblance of peace and order returned when Captain Antonio Gil Ybarbo incorporated Nacogdches in 1779 under the flag of Spain. He built a two-story house called the Old Stone House. It was also used as a fort on occasion. The town was populated by Indians and Spanish alike. A few Anglos entered the area around Nacogdoches and Ayish Bayou.

It was not until the turn of the century that the Anglos started coming in force. First they followed the Irishman Phillip Nolan, and then Dr. James Long and his group of filibusters. Texas was changed forever.

The Magee-Gutiérrez Expedition between 1812 and 1820 again ran most of the Mexican and Anglo settlers out of East Texas. Lieutenant Augustus Magee, United States Army, graduate of West Point, stationed at Fort Jessup, Louisiana, resigned his commission to join Don José Bernardo Maximiliano Gutiérrez de Lora in his fight against Spanish rule. They named their army the "Republican Army of the North." They meant North Mexico, but the name stuck in the minds of the

Spanish and Mexicans for years. The North meant the United States. The Magee-Gutiérrez Expidition was crushed.

The Spanish kept East Texas clear of all Anglo Settlers, except for a few hardy souls. When Mexico won its independence from Spain in 1821, the new government of Mexico sent Erasmus Seguín to Nacogdoches. All the old Mexican and Anglo settlers were invited back to their homes.

Things were quiet until 1825, when the Mexican Government gave Haden Edwards an empresario contract for land south of the old Camino Real and just east of the Sabine River. His son-in-law, Frost Thorn, was given a contract for land north of the Camino and Nacogdoches at the same time. Thorn did not bring families into his grant, feeling that the Indians already present on the land were better farmers and hide hunters than the whites. He was interested in commerce, not political power.

But Edwards and his brother, Benjamin, were interested in political power. That meant they must have their own people on their land. But there were already settlers on this land, most of whom were Mexican. Edwards tried to expel the old settlers. This caused a fuss in Mexico City and he was told to step down, or else. Edwards, at the urging of his brother Benjamin, decided to start a revolution, which became the Fredonian Rebellion. Again much of East Texas was cleared of many of its settlers, most fleeing across the Sabine River.

Things settled down when Stephen Prather, ex-captain in Andrew Jackson's army, left his Indian trading post near Bevil's Diggings with his former comrade-at-arms from the War of 1812 Milton Hicks, five other white men, and about sixty Indians, and broke up the rebellion. The rebelling white men were drunk in their camp when Prather and his group arrived. The Indians, war paint and all, gave out a few blood-curdling whoops and the Army of the Rebellion surrendered without a shot being fired. That was in 1826.

The Mexican Government sent Colonel José de las Piedras to command the Nacogdoches Military District and see that there were no more uprisings led by Anglos from the North. It had taken the colonel and his command, half of his men being made up of former criminals, only two years to bring disgust and hate from both Mexican and Anglo settler alike. His men stole without fear of punishment and Piedras himself was a tyrant.

This was the climate of East Texas in that spring day of 1829 when Milton Hicks, English-Cherokee Indian breed, went after Thumping Turtle, the Spanish-Coushatta Indian breed.

Chapter Four

Milton stood over six feet four inches. He got his height from his Cherokee ancestors, along with his black hair. His face was free of hair and he followed the Cherokee custom of plucking his eyebrows of all hair. This in itself would mark him as an American Indian if a person was observing. The skin that was exposed to the hot sun and wind was tanned a deep brown. But he was not much darker than many sunburned and windblown white men of the frontier. His huge, large-boned frame was void of all fat, held together by tough muscle and sinew. His blue eyes came from his English great-grandfather Nathan Hicks, an English trader from the Virginia Colony who had married into the tribe in 1766. Nathan had married Nayehi, "One-who-goes-about," of the Ani-waya, "Wolf Clan," and a member of the most powerful family in the Cherokee Nation.

With his quarter English blood, his admixture of American Indian and Anglo frontiersman garb, he looked like any other frontiersman. Except there was something wild and different about this man that set him apart from others.

He was a warrior and he had learned his trade as the grandson of Tsali Usgasit, "Fierce Charlie," known to the whites and history as Charles Hicks. Charles Hicks had been principal chief of the Cherokee Nation when he died two years before in 1827. He had long been buried before Milton had learned of his death. It was said that in his lifetime Chief Hicks had been the most influential and powerful man among the Cherokee. Not even such fierce old warriors as Major Ridge and Doublehead would buck Chief Hicks.

Milton had joined Andrew Jackson's Army in the War of 1812 as a member of the Cherokee Regiment to fight against the Red Sticks. After the Battle of Horseshoe Bend, the rest of the Cherokee went home. Milton and a few other Cherokee went west with Jackson's Army to New Orleans. Two years after the Battle of New Orleans he came to Texas. He had found a liking for the smell of fresh blood and gunpowder, the excitement of adventure. Milton Hicks would go anywhere to follow the gun.

The tall man clad in leather breeches, knee-high moccasins, called shoe-boots by the Cherokee, and buckskin shirt, rode into Nacogdoches on the afternoon of the third day. He rode in, looking at the increasing size of the town. New buildings were going up everywhere. Many of the old buildings were being repaired and moved into. He had heard that there were over four hundred people in the town alone, half being Mexican and half being Yanquis from the States. Indians from the different tribes of East Texas were in town for trade. There were more people living on the immediate outskirts of the town.

The town was noisy beyond belief. White men, both the Mexican and the Anglo, were yellers. Indians had learned to sit and listen to the noise without covering their ears with their hands.

Houses were being built along North Street, a centuries-old road used by Indians of the past. Some of the houses were of Mexican frontier design known as a *jacal*. They were constructed by driving pickets or stakes into the ground and fastening them on top by a plate which supported a simple gabled roof. The spaces between the poles were plastered with clay and the roofline was extended to protect the walls from rain. There was a small opening for a door and there were usually no windows. A dwelling might contain no more than one or two rooms. Every home had a stick-and-mud chimney, which both heated the home and provided a cooking place.

The Anglos had brought their style of log house to Texas

with them. Most of them had one room, one door, no windows, like those of their Mexican neighbors. This type of log house was no better or worse than the Mexican *jacal*, just different.

There were a few rock homes, the stone being quarried from Banita and La Nana creeks.

Rich Anglos built frame houses. Lumber usually came from the sawmills of Peter Ellis Bean or from John Durst. Slaves made shanks for roof shingles.

Although slavery was against Mexican law, an exception was made for the Anglos who already owned slaves. No slaves could be bought or sold in Mexico, by anyone. Free slaves had the same privileges as any white person.

Two buildings towered above all of the others in the small town. One was the Casa Piedra, the Old Stone House, that had been built by Captain Antonio Gil Ybarbo around 1780. John Durst now lived on the upper floor and his store occupied the first floor. The second house was the three-story frame house on Main Street that had been built in 1825 by wealthy Frost Thorn for his new bride, Susan Edwards.

People paused to watch Milton pass.

Milton rode around the Plaza Principal and up to Thorn's mercantile. He stepped from his horse. The horse immediately lowered a hip to stand relaxed and hipshot at the hitching post. Both of his ears flopped back and forth, then dropped on each side of his head with an appearance of dejection. Milton had gotten the Plains Indian war horse a year before. They were just now getting to like each other. But the little Indian pony did not like anyone else.

The tall breed looked across the Plaza at the Red House, home and office of Colonel Piedras. The house got its name from the adobe made from the local red soil to plaster its outer walls. His eyes darted next to the Catholic Church that was now being used to garrison the Mexican troops of Piedras's command. Always the hunter, be it of man or animal, he was continuously checking and evaluating his surroundings.

Milton walked into the mercantile, his long Pennsylvania-made "Kentucky rifle" in the crook of his arm. A pistol was stuck in his belt with his favorite weapon, the tomahawk. He also carried a new large-bladed Bowie knife that Jim Bowie had given him the year before.

As he stepped through the door from the bright sunlit afternoon to the darkened interior of this store, he automatically stepped to one side of the opening to wait for his eyes to adjust to the light.

The storekeeper looked up as Milton stepped into the room. He saw the stern eyes that peered from under the standard broad-brimmed, floppy felt hat of the frontiersman of Texas. The older man was Haden Edwards, a formerly wealthy man from Virginia who had lost everything in the Fredonian Rebellion. He was now a junior partner in his son-in-law's mercantile business.

"How do, Milton?" Haden greeted him.

"Fine, Haden. How do?" returned Milton.

"Okay, for an old man. Expected to see you comin' this way," Haden told him.

"Pete tell you I'd come?" asked Milton.

"Yep."

"Damned sure of himself," Milton said.

Haden grinned. "He knows you."

"Yeah, I reckon," admitted Milton.

"He said for us to give you anything you wanted for a possible long stay," Haden informed him.

"Long as there ain't no casket involved," Milton said dryly. Milton handed him a slip of paper. "Got it all down here on paper."

"Let's see who you be after," reflected Haden. "There's five different Indians loose that the law's after. Ain't none but one they'd send Milton Hicks to git. That'd be Thumping Turtle."

Milton made no comment.

Haden Edwards knew that Milton was going after only Indians. He could not conceive that anyone would send a breed after a white man, not even a breed as well liked and respected as Milton Hicks. He had still not gotten used to the idea that Mexicans thought of an Indian as just another citizen. It was doubtful that he would ever change.

"Haden H., take this bill and fill it for Mister Hicks," Hayden ordered his youngest son.

Haden H. signaled a "Howdy" to Milton and took the bill from his father.

"Milton, Frost is in his office. Would you come in and talk with us?" asked Haden.

"Reckon so," Milton agreed.

Milton followed Haden back to a rear office. Without formalities Haden walked into the room.

"What's up, Papa?" asked a heavyset man behind a desk. "Ah, Milton Hicks."

"How do, Mr. Thorn?" greeted Milton.

"Just fine. I seen you're okay and still have your hair," Frost said with a grin. He did not offer a hand to Milton. The breed was not the handshaking type.

Frost was of medium height, a stocky man who was becoming portly in his thirty-sixth year. But he was not a soft man. There was strength in the New Yorker. A strength that had made him a wealthy man in New Orleans and the wealthiest man in Texas. His power and influence did not come only because of his social and economic standing. He was an intelligent man to deal with and he was honest and straightforward to a fault. He could be counted on to stand with his friends. That meant more than money in this part of the world.

"We heard you might be coming through," said Frost.

"He's going after Thumping Turtle," Haden informed Frost.

Frost raised his eyebrows.

"It should be a good 'un," grinned Haden.

"I'll have to agree to that," said Frost. "Especially since he's reported to have gone east and is with that border trash in the ld Neutral Zone. Hell, there's about as many outlaws b tween the Ayish Bayou settlement and the Sabine on the Texas side as well as the Louisiana side."

"We do have a few here in Texas," agreed Haden.

"I like interestin' livin'," replied Milton with the hint of a smile. "Your pack train saw him over there?"

"Yes, that's where I got my reports," Frost told him. He poured three glasses of Scotch and handed one to Milton and one to his father-in-law. They toasted "Here's to Texas." Milton drank as if he enjoyed the stuff.

"Milton, while you're moving around out in the Neutral, keep your eyes and ears open. See what the Americans are up to. See if you can learn about any military forces forming within striking distance of Texas," suggested Frost. "All of us would like to know where the Americans stand."

"Hell, we know how they stand!" said Haden. He poured himself another drink.

"Papa," complained Frost, "we want to know as many details as we can find."

"Yeah, you're right," admitted Haden. "I'd rather see Texas a republic than part of the U.S. under that man in the White House right now."

"I'm being paid by Pete. You know I'll tell him everything I tell you," Milton assured them.

"That's fine with us. We're not with those Anglos over in Ayish Bayou or Liberty area who want to make Texas part of the States. Most of the old settlers here don't," Frost told Milton. "Listen to what people's got to say, if anything, while you're on the road. It's good business to keep an eye on the east."

"I'll see what I can find out," Milton promised. He didn't want to see an influx of Anglos coming into Mexico either.

"If you get in a tight spot and need a place in Louisiana, go to Natchitoches. I still have a house there," Frost offered. He took out his quill and wrote a note on paper. "Give this to my black there and tell him to put you up, find you a lawyer, or anything else you need."

"I don't reckon I'll need it, but I'll take it just in case," Milton told him. "One other thing: Piedras don't know I'm going, does he?"

"No, just a few of us," replied Frost. He knew Milton's feelings for the Mexican Army officer.

"Good. I just couldn't spy for that man. He's too damned nervous to be in command on the frontier," Milton stated, knowing that this was one of the few things he could out-wardly seem emotional about. He left, calling over his shoulder, "I'll pick up those things later, Mr. Edwards."

"They'll be ready," Haden informed him.

Haden looked at his son-in-law. "How long do you think we got before the Americans come in?"

"Less than ten years," observed Frost. "The Americans didn't buy all that Louisiana land for nothing. They want to expand, and expand they will. Not Mexico, we frontiersmen, Indians, or anyone else is going to stop them from reaching the Pacific."

"Yeah, reckon you're right," Haden drawled. There was a conflict of accents when these two started talking. There was a New York Long Island sound mixed with the southern drawl of Virginia.

"It's a curse of the European who has come to the New World, we want to expand," Frost reminded the older man. "Hell, Papa, that's why we came. Old King Jackson is going to be nipping at this Texas thing until it's done. We're going to hear rumor after rumor about him wanting Texas. That'll scare hell out of men like Piedras. We're in for a rough time these next few years."

"King Jackson? You sound like a Whig," laughed Haden.

"I don't like one-man rule. Jackson and his Democrats do," said Frost. "Most important of all, I don't trust politicians and American frontiersmen when it comes to expansion. If you'll notice, King Jackson is both."

"Maybe you're right," admitted Haden.

"We live in troubled times, Papa. We'll have very little peace during our lives."

"I ain't had much yet." Haden gave a bitter laugh.

Milton led his horse to Goyens's stable. If he was going to spend the night in Nacogdoches, he might as well have his horse fed and rubbed down by the best. If he could find anyone to do it. He had one mean horse.

William Goyens was known, liked, and respected by all in Nacogdoches. He was a mulatto from North Carolina with a free black father and a white mother. As a free black he'd been able to leave the United States and come to Mexico where he would have a chance for advancement.

Will had arrived in Texas about 1825, and in that four years had gained a smithy, hostelry, a wagon-making shop, a gun shop, an inn, and he was accumulating a large tract of land. Next to Frost Thorn, Adolphus Sterne, and the Durst brothers, he was the wealthiest and most prominent man in the Nacogdoches area.

Goyens was an intelligent man who could read and write both English and Spanish, and spoke both languages, plus French and a couple of Indian languages. He had argued a number of cases in court for friends, winning more than he lost.

Will came out of the blacksmith's as Milton walked up. "Well, well, Mister Milton Hicks in person. Done come to town to be with us civilized folks. How do, Milton?"

"Fine, Will. Horse needs tending. How about a hoof check and trim by your boys?" asked Milton.

"That's a goddamned mean hoss you got there, Milton," Will said, eyeing him over.

"You get extra for every rib he breaks." Milton smiled. "I got ridin' to do, so do what's necessary."

"Put it on Bean's government account?" Will asked.

Milton nodded his head. Hell! Everybody knew he was coming through Nacogdoches and why. All except Piedras. They sure kept him in the dark. Most nobody talked to that man.

"You hear all that, Isaac?" Will asked a black man.

"Yas, suh, Mistuh Will. I do it rat now, but I tole you now, Mistuhs, I shore 'fraid of thet hoss," Isaac complained.

"You do the best you can," Will told him. "I'll send help."

"Is thet the same hoss you stole from thet Comanche Indian, Mistuh Hicks?" asked Isaac.

"It's the same one," grinned Milton, taking off the saddle.

"Oh, Lawdy, Lawdy, Mistuh Will, sends lots of help," Isaac begged.

"I'll do it, Isaac," Will promised. "Why do you keep that damned thing, Milton?"

"It took me a month to be able to saddle him without a fight each time. It took three months 'afore I could get in the saddle without him havin' a damned fit an' tryin' to buck me off. I got too much tied up in him."

"See what you mean," said Will, not sure he agreed with the reasoning.

Isaac walked around the horse. The more he looked at the horse, the more appreciative his expression grew, mixed in with a large dose of apprehension. He said, "Mistah Hicks, you got yo'self a fine hoss. That critter be a real stayer. He be one fine hoss. But I still don' lak to mess wit him."

"If Isaac says he's a fine hoss, then he be one," replied Will.

"Yas, suh, Mistah Will, if'n this nigger tell ya a hoss is a good un, you kin sho believe it," Isaac told him.

Isaac walked up near the head of the horse and it bared its teeth at him. Isaac told the horse, "Look heah, hoss, me an' you is gonna be friens. Ain't no use in us'uns fightin'."

"You got somethin' to keep that hoss from chewin' old Isaac up?" Will asked Milton.

"Yep. I've got this rawhide halter that slips over his head and down over his muzzle." Milton pulled it from his gear. "It's small looking, but it's strong and will clamp that mouth shut."

"That's an Indian rig, ain't it?" Will asked, a pattern for a potential rig of his own already going through his mind.

"My granddaddy gave it to me," Milton told him. "As for his feet, Isaac, I sure do hope you're fast on yours."

"I think I is today, Mistah Hicks," Isaac assured him.

Milton slipped the rawhide halter over the horse's head and pulled the loop up tight. "If he kills somebody, let me know."

"Lawd, if'n he kill somebody, it gonna be this nigger," Isaac told Milton. "I won't git nobody to help me."

Milton handed the rope to Isaac. As soon as he let go, the horse came unwound.

Isaac hung on and yelled, "I's sho glad you doan come to town offen, Mistah Hicks, an' tha's fo' a fact."

Isaac and the horse made a charge in the barn, the big black man a half a step ahead of the horse. A crash was heard from the interior and a loud "Lawd, hoss, I's be yo frien', goddammit!"

"Maybe I should stay and help him," Milton told Will.

"Isaac don't need no help. He be the best hoss handler you ever saw," Will assured him. "That hoss'll be meek as a baby lamb come morning."

"Ain't nobody that good," Milton told Will.

"It'd be my pleasure to buy you a drink," Will told Milton.

"Be pleased," he replied, then he yelled, "Isaac, don't you hurt my hoss!"

"Oh, no, suh, I doan hurt him. But I sho already got some hurts fo myself," Isaac returned.

Milton and Will left the hostelry.

"I saw that big, beautiful rifle of yours an' I see you still got the flint system. Why don't you come by an' let me change it over to a percussion?" Will asked him. They tipped their hats to the ladies on the street.

"I'm kinda used to the old flint," Milton told him. It was hard to change.

"I tell you, them percussions is the comin' thing. You can have your percussion caps separate, don't even have to keep 'em in your action. If it rains, then you don't get the thing wet. When you need it, put her in an' *bam!* You got a good fire."

"Sounds pretty good. I've seen 'em before," Milton said, still not sure if he wanted to change.

"Come by when you got time an' I'll show you the better of the two systems. Then you'll have something to think on," urged Will.

Milton agreed that he would.

Chapter Five

Milton and Will met a man coming toward them on the street. He approached them with a smile of acknowledgment.

"Well, Will, it look like you done caught yourself an Indian," Adolphus Sterne said in his thick German accent. The German Jew looked as if he had stepped off the streets of his native Cologne, Germany. He was another one of those admixtures that made up frontier Texas. His father was an Orthodox Jew and his mother a Lutheran. As a citizen of Mexico, he was legally a convert to Catholicism. That was a good thing about the state of Texas, Mexico—no one much cared about your background.

This man commanded respect no matter what company he found himself in. He had a friendly respect for his fellow man that everyone enjoyed participating in freely. He was a trader and owned a *mercantile*.

"Who do, Mr. Sterne?" greeted Milton.

"You have a busy day?" asked Will.

"Ya, pretty busy. Some Indians come into the store. They speak of the future crops they be plantin'. They say they be pretty good, ya," Dolf told them. He laughed, "We all make money."

Making money was the dearest thing to a merchant's heart.

The afternoon was late and the street was crowded with people on their way home at the end of the day.

Vicente Cordova, native born in Nacogdoches, from a family of old Spanish settlers, joined them. He was captain of the local militia and had served as alcalde, primary judge, and regidor of Nacogdoches. He was invited to join them in a drink.

Before they got to Sim's Saloon on the Plaza, the crowd was getting too large to suit Milton. These were town people. They loved a crowd and talking, but this child of the forest did not.

The men were friendly and the rum and beer flowed freely. The talk flowed back and forth about Mexican politics, the Indian situation in the southeastern United States, the Indian situation in Mexico, and in Texas in particular.

These men had come to the conclusion long ago that if there were any real problems with the Indians, it would be caused by white men. When they looked back over the years, they had had no real problems with Indians. At least not in the East Texas area. The only Indian problem they ever had was with individual Indians themselves. But most of the "big" problems with the Indian nations were in the minds of the whites. If you wanted to stir up trouble or gain some more land, all a person had to do was spread the word that the Indians were getting ready to go on the warpath and kill all the white people west of the Sabine River and north of the Río Bravo. Then the hysteria would take charge and rumors would fly from one end of Texas to the other like wildfire. There was one way to determine that there was no trouble in East Texas. All a person had to do was look around him. If the Indians ever decided to go on the warpath and kill all the white people, there would not be a white person left alive.

These men worried more about the Anglos of the North than they did about Indians. They had lived with Indians all of their lives. But they knew they could not live with the Anglos from the North. Most Anglos lived around you, not with you. There was a difference.

This was the talk in the saloon.

Milton sat and listened, gathering information from all sides.

Haden Edwards joined them around the huge table that was always used by the locals.

Charles Stanfield Taylor, native of London, England, and a new arrival to Texas, joined them. The new citizen was a boarder of Dolf Sterne.

"Now that Andy Jackson is President, no tellin' which way Texas is gonna go," growled Haden. "To hell in a basket, I reckon. We be in a bad time, friends and gentlemen."

"That's for certain sure," agreed Dolf.

"Do you know what Frost calls Jackson?" Haden laughed.

"Ain't much tellin', but I bet it's with class," said Will.

"If he's ticked off at a fellow, then he ain't got no class," Haden told him. "He can put more goddamns in than a mule drover."

"What does he call Jackson?" asked Dolf, not knowing or much caring about U.S. politics.

"He calls ole' Andy 'King Jackson.'" Haden laughed again.

"By God, that do make a good description of him," agreed Will.

"Better than what I call him," Milton commented for the first time.

"Milton, you was in his army a couple of years fightin' again' the Red Sticks. What say you?" asked Charles, curious about the opinions of a man who personally knew the President of America.

"We watched him close like. He sure didn't mind sendin' his Indian auxiliaries into the front doors of the slaughterhouse," Milton said dryly.

"He did have a rough time gettin' a victory before he won a good un of his own at New Orleans, didn't he?" observed Haden.

"Yep, that's for a fact. I was at the Battle of Talladega in thirteen," Milton informed them.

"You was just a young critter, weren't you?" asked Haden.

"Fourteen, maybe fifteen. Me an' a cousin went with the

Cherokee scouts when the war first started," said Milton. War was a subject he was comfortable with.

"The cousin come to Texas with you?" inquired Charles.

"Nope. Left him on the banks of the Tallapoosa. He went the way of a warrior, so he wasn't sad," Milton informed them. "I sang his war song for him an' sent him on his way to the west."

"You was with Jackson in most of the battles, weren't you?" asked Haden.

"I was in a hell of a lot more than he was. We, the Indians and breeds, saved his bacon many times. It sure hurt his ole' soul and pride. That's one of the reasons he hates the red man so. That an' because his land speculation deals of the red man's land went sour." Milton laughed. This was one of Milton's few joys, knowing that Jackson had lost money on Indian land.

"He didn't depend on Indians that much." It's hard to say a white man needs some help against the little brown man. The man was an outsider, standing away from the group. He was ignored.

"We nearly lost that battle at Talladega in thirteen. Jackson an' his men weren't the best soldiers I ever seen," Milton told them. "There were about one hundred and fifty of us, Indians and breeds, at the Creek town of Talladega. The scouts discovered six hundred Red Sticks near us, just waiting for the right time. They didn't know it had already passed. Word was sent to Jackson that the Red Sticks had been found. He marched in with about two thousand men with cannon. Jackson drew the Red Sticks in and tried to use the same tactics as Hannibal at the Battle of Cannae, but—"

"The who done what where?" asked Will.

"He is correct. Milton is a student of history an' a widely read man," Dolf put in.

"When Jackson closed the circle, the Red Sticks went wild. They broke the line in the white men's area. The white men ran, nearly gettin' all of us killed. The men ran, cryin' that their enlistment was up an' they was goin' home." Milton gave a semigrowl. "We, the Indians, held and fought. We killed about three hundred Red Sticks that day. We lost about fifteen killed and eighty-five wounded."

"Is it right the Red Sticks used bows and arrows, seldom guns?" asked Will.

"Yep. An' they was always outnumbered by at least two to one in every battle. But like I said, Jackson an' his men weren't the best soldiers I ever seen," Milton told them again. "In fourteen, on the banks of the Emukfau Creek that runs into the Tallapoosa, we were attacked by Red Sticks. There were about sixty-five Cherokees and two hundred White Sticks along. But ole' Chicken Snake never used the Indian properly as scouts. All the Indians were at Jackson's rear when the attack started. Jackson was bein' beat bad. We fought our way up to the front an' held off the attack so Jackson an' his army could escape. There weren't really that many Red Sticks thet day. Ole Andy an' his boys took off for Fort Strother. General Coffee was bein' carried on a litter, him bein' wounded. Jackson's army hit the crossin' at Enotachopco Creek, an' guess who caught them by surprise? The same damned Creek Red Sticks that'd chewed 'em up at Tallapoosa. We finally caught up with Jackson again. Between us and Jackson's nine pounder shootin' grapeshot, we were able to break contact an' make it to Fort Strother."

Milton paused and downed the rest of his beer. Dolf ordered another round.

Milton continued. "The thing about that fight, there weren't no more than five hundred Creeks in the whole damned battle. Here we had two thousand or more. Jackson didn't use his men right, an' his men wouldn't stand an' fight."

"Gawddamn!" exclaimed Will.

"Yeah, ole Stephen Prather can shore git kickin' mad talkin' about it," laughed Haden.

"You oughta hear ole Brit Bailey down Brazoria way," Milton informed him.

"That battle you just described, wasn't far from where the battle of Horseshoe Bend was fought, was it?" Charles asked.

"Nope, just down the river a piece. Horseshoe was fought in March of fourteen, 'bout three months before. It was a battle, all right. If it hadn't been for the Indians guidin' the soldiers into position, then swimming the river to get Creek canoes to cross over to the island the Red Sticks were on, Jackson wouldn't a won that battle. Or slaughter, I should say," Milton told them. He hadn't talked himself out yet. "There were about six hundred Cherokees and three or four hundred Creek White Sticks and Yuchi warriors. Jackson still had an army of two thousand white soldiers. The Red Sticks had about nine hundred, all told. When the battle was over, there was about three hundred women and children left alive. No count of dead women and children was ever taken. Of the nine hundred Red Sticks, about seventy lived."

"Seventy?" asked Charles, impressed.

"Yep. They was quite an honorable bunch—warriors," Milton told them. "All the ole Cherokee warriors said they was the among the best, which is high praise comin' from a Cherokee."

More beer and rum were ordered. Listening caused as big a thirst as talking.

Milton wiped the warm suds from his mouth and continued, "We had forty-nine killed in our army. Twenty-three of them were Indians. Of the one hundred and fifty-four who were wounded, forty-seven were Indians."

"Are you counted with the red men?" Charles the Britisher wanted to know.

"Yep, with the red. Red men will accept my white blood. White Americans won't accept my red blood," Milton told him.

Milton finished his story and tried to back out of the picture, as was his habit.

He had impressed the men around the table. None had ever heard him speak at such length before.

Haden tried one more time at pulling Milton back in the circle. "Ole Andy did it on his own in New Orleans, didn't he?"

"That he did. Whipped hell outta the British. Stopped 'em cold." The tall man looked at Charles Taylor and grinned. "Of course, gentlemen, they ain't Indians."

Taylor laughed with them.

The men were enjoying their rum, beer, and company.

A man started past their table, when he looked down at Will Goyens. "Hey, ain't you a nigger?"

The men looked up at the Anglo standing before them, balancing on unsteady legs.

"You," he called, pointing at Will, "ain't you a nigger?"

"Half of me is. Has been all my life," Will told him.

"Wal, I don't drink with niggers," the man exclaimed.

"Today you is lucky. Only the white half is drinkin'," Will told him lightly.

"Not only thet, you is a smart-ass nigger," the man growled.

"I suggest you go someplace else to drink, sir," said Dolf.

"Back in North Carolina we don't drink with no niggers or dogs," the man said.

Now, where have I heard that before? thought Milton, getting ready for the action that would come.

"That's the reason I left North Carolina," Will told the man.

Two friends joined the Anglo. Their legs were as whiskey shaky as their friend's.

"We do not wish trouble. We drink as friends, with friends," Dolf told the man.

"Hey, ain't you some kinda foreigner?" the man asked.

"No, sir, you are the foreigner here. This man is a citizen of Mexico," Vicente said in broken English.

The Anglos growled. They were tough. They were mean. They wanted a fight.

"Mister, I ain't no goddamned foreigner no place I go," the first man said through gritted teeth.

"Here in Texas you are a foreigner. And you are in my country and in my town. I am the captain of the militia here. The militia takes my commands," Vicente told him. "Now. Do you wish to hear my commands?"

The man stood swaying slightly, his eyes hard and his jaw set. He hated to back down. The taste was bad. It was especially hard to back down to an inferior Mexican. But he knew the price he and his friends might have to pay if they pressed themselves upon these men. That price would be even more bitter than a simple loss of face. He had heard how Mexicans treated prisoners and he wanted none of that.

The men did not see the real threat, which was sitting in the background, watching all of this with keen interest. That threat was Milton Hicks, who was calm on the outside but wound up tight and ready to act. He felt this night might not be so boring after all.

The Anglo suddenly relaxed. The excitement was over. All that was left now was the talking. Milton could do without that.

"We don't let niggers get away with acting like they was as good as white folks back in the States," the first man said.

"You Mexicans air gonna be sorry lettin' them darkies an' Injuns act just lak white folks," put in the second man.

"Yeah, even you Meskins think yore somebody," the third added his two cents.

"I think you three oughta mosey right on outta here. Then you can get your horses and move right on outta town. Maybe even Mexico," an Anglo behind them said.

The men turned and one asked, "Just who the hell you think you air?"

"A man who just got to Texas," the man told him. "I aim to set up shop here, so I don't want trash like you three stinking up the place."

"We don't gotta take that goddamned kinda talk," the second man sputtered.

There was a smile on Vicente's face when he told them,

"My friend, you are now in a position that's called a crossfire. It is a very bad position to be in. In fact, it is a deadly position to be in."

The three Anglos stood a moment, judging the situation. They decided it prudent to back down. They were not that good or that drunk.

"You better hope we don't meet on the trail somewhere," the first man growled at the interfering Anglo. He had to have a parting shot before he left.

"Look for me any time. Ask for Wes Johnson. It will be my pleasure," Johnson assured him.

Vicente pointed to the door, not saying a thing.

The three men left.

"Say, Mister Johnson, join us," offered Will.

"No, thank you, gentlemen. I have an early start," he told them. His accent was southern, his manners polite.

"Might I ask where you be going?" asked Haden.

"Down to Austin's Colony," Johnson informed them.

"He's a goodun, all right," said Will.

"That he is," agreed Vicente.

"Goodnight, gentlemen," Johnson said as he left.

The men watched him walk out.

"Now, Texas can use more Anglos like that man," said Dolf.

"Agreed," said Vicente.

Milton stood up to leave.

"The drinking just started, Milton," Vicente informed him.

"Yeah, but I got an early start and long road on my hands come morning," Milton replied. He downed the rest of his beer and got to his feet.

"You will pay, dammit!" a man's voice broke through the noise.

"Sounds like ole Sim is having soldier trouble again," replied Haden.

"When I get paid, I pay you," the Mexican soldier told Sim.

"Like hell! I want it now! You people go six or seven months without gettin' paid," Sim boomed. "I need bein' paid now!"

"Nine," the soldier told him.

"Nine? Nine what?" Sim yelled.

"Since we get paid," the soldier told him.

"Goddamn, any of you could be sent to hell 'afore I got my money," Sim told him.

"Sir, I'm already in hell. I am in East Texas," the soldier shot back.

Sim stood a moment. Then he shook his head helplessly. "Get the hell outta here!"

The soldier left, holding the half-full bottle in his hand.

The saloon relaxed with a sigh of relief. Drunk soldiers had been known to come back in force and tear up a place, arresting everyone in it. It would be morning before the arrogant little army colonel would redress the injustice of his troops.

"You can stay at the inn. I got room. If I don't, I make room," Will told Milton.

"Don't like beds. Too damned soft," Milton complained. *And I don't care for towns*, followed in his mind.

"I got a hard woman that might please you. She's black as coal," Will offered him. It was as ironic as the times. Will, a free black, in a free country, owned slaves.

Milton grinned with the rest of the men. He left the saloon with his normal wave of a hand.

Chapter Six

Milton picked up his bedroll and weapons at Goyen's stables. Gear swung over his shoulder he made his way to the campgrounds west of town on Arroyo Bañita, or "Little Bath Creek." He stayed clear of the campfires of other travelers and spread his bedroll under the shadows of an old oak tree.

The moon was bright and he watched people go back and forth between fires. It looked as if it might be clear tonight with no rain.

Texas was getting crowded, to his way of thinking. Settlers were coming down the Old San Antonio Road from Natchitoches, Louisiana, every week. Soon half the Americans in the United States would be in Texas, trying to outrun the bad economy of the United States or to seek adventure. With the Anglos would come their brand of civilization. With their brand of civilization there would be no room for men such as Milton Hicks. In Mexican Texas he was not considered an Indian breed. He was considered a man. A man who was good with a gun and good to have in a fight. A man could ride the river with Milton Hicks and be damned sure that if anything went wrong, he would ride into the river to save him.

The Mexicans were not like the Anglos of the North. Most of them were colorblind when it came to race. A man such as Will Goyens had a chance to develop into the outstanding businessman and craftsman he was. That was something he could not do in the United States. Not even in the north, unless he had a white person backing him. Here in Texas he could do what he wanted. Milton liked Mexico.

The figure of a woman went from bedroll to bedroll. She

did not go the the fires, but kept to the edges of the camp-ground. She knew who she was looking for.

"Milton?" she called.

Milton lay quiet. He knew the woman. She was young and a little on the plump side for a Cherokee, but what the hell? He had been a few nights without a woman.

"Milton?" the woman called again.

"Over here," Milton answered softly.

"Ah, there you are, you scoundrel," she said, laughter in her voice. She crawled under his canvas rain cover. She squirmed a moment and then she was out of her clothes.

"Glad to feel you, Francisca," he told her.

She felt of him and found that he was still in his buckskin pants.

"You have clothes on, blackhearted scoundrel," she complained, pulling at the cord to undo his pants.

"You need a bath," he told her bluntly.

"Oh, you make me so mad. Mad, mad, mad! Always a bath. You are the cleanest man I know. No, you are the cleanest person I know. You bathe everyday," she complained.

"Twice a day, when I got the water. Every morning at sunrise, and every evening. Bathing is good for you. Water cleanses your body and your soul. It's a purifier," he told her.

"Anglos don't bathe that often. Most I know bathes only when it rains." She pouted.

"I'm Cherokee and Anglo. The Cherokee part takes the baths," he assured her.

"I'm Spanish and Comanche. We don't bathe. They don't got no water out there," she informed him, rubbing him between the legs. She still didn't get a rise out of him.

"True. Out there, water is scarce. But we're here, not there, so git."

She sighed and stood up, wrapping the blanket around her nakedness. "You go with me. A man may come after my virginity if he sees me naked in the water."

"Pity the man who tries to rape Francisca Ruis." Milton chuckled.

He followed her to the creek. She was splashing around in the water before he got there. He sat on the bank of the river and chewed on a dried apple he had found in town.

Francisca got out of the water and threw herself in his lap. She was wet, but she smelled better. She kissed him and rubbed a hand over his bare chest.

He wrapped the blanket around her and picked her up in his arms. He carried her back to his bedroll.

"I thought you were married again," he told her.

"Husbands are under every bush on the frontier," she informed him. She pulled him down to her, covering their nakedness with the blanket. "Besides, I never knew an Anglo or a Cherokee who worried about a husband in the background."

"Just as long as he doesn't have a bead on me," he admitted.

"Ha! Wouldn't you fight for my affections?" she demanded.

"Not for yours or no other woman's," he told her. Then he asked, "What will you tell the priest tomorrow?"

"That I dreamed I was made love to by a bronze god. Now, do it! We will talk later." She giggled.

They were safely locked in their own world, ignoring the rest of the universe around them.

Milton woke well before dawn. The moon was down, leaving the stars to light the world with their feeble glow. The world was wet from the heavy dew and mist of the morning. Fog hung in the low places.

He went to the creek and bathed in the water. After his bath he dipped under the water seven times, facing the east. Old habits and customs were hard to break, especially when no one else was around to see you.

When he finished, he returned to the camp and picked up his gear. He departed quietly, leaving Francisca rolled in the blanket. He had another lighter blanket that would be better in the coming heat.

He left a trail in the dew as he crossed the predawn wet grass.

Isaac woke after the second call. He climbed down from the hayloft where he slept. "I figured you'd be here early as always. I got yore stuff from the sto' lak you said."

"Thanks, Isaac," Milton told him. "I like early morning best. You get to see the birth of a sun on a new day."

Isaac looked at him for a moment while he made sure his pants were buttoned. "I know'd you got soul, Mistuh Milton. I could always feel it. You don' talks too much, but when you do, you say soul things."

Milton figured that for a great compliment.

"How did you an' that hoss make out?" Milton asked.

"Wow, an' Lawd, Lawd! I'm gonna show you, Mistuh Milton," Isaac told him, pulling off his slipover shirt. He pointed to some scratches and bruises. "That hoss don thet."

He slipped down his pants to show more battle scars. There was a large dark-purple imprint of a horse's hoof on the outer thigh of his dark leg. "Lawd, Lawd, I shore wuz glad he couldn't bite."

"Did he ever settle down?" asked Milton.

"Oh, shore did, suh, jest as soon as I left. He settles down right peaceable like," Isaac assured him, then laughed with pleasure. "One o' 'em young uppity niggers of Mistuh Thorn's come by with some yaller gal. You know them house niggers can git them yaller gals. He wuz gonna be a smart-ass and show dis gal how much he know'd 'bout them hosses. I seed him and tole him them hosses gets downright mean if'n anybody messed with 'em while they wuz on their feed. I pointed to yo hoss stall an' says he's the worst of 'em all."

Isaac laughed, pulling up his pants and placing his shirttail inside. "Wal, Mistuh Milton, that uppity nigger walked right into thet stall jest as bold as brass. Thet ole hoss, he jest stood an' didn't bat an eye. Jest kept on munchin' his feed. All a sudden thet hoss come after thet nigger. Bust through the gate an' chased him down the aisle an' bit him a good un on the butt. Din thet ole hoss turns around and moseys on back to his stall."

Milton grinned while Isaac laughed and slapped his legs.

"I'll saddle him, Isaac," Milton told him.

"Lawdy, Mistuh Milton, I sho' would thank ya."

Milton saddled the horse and led him out of the barn. The horse eyed Isaac. The black man kept his distance.

"Ain't nobody never gonna steal thet hoss off'n you," Isaac assured Milton.

Milton grinned.

"Mistuh Milton, you be after thet big buck, Thumpin' Turtle?" Isaac asked.

"I be," Milton told him.

"He be heah a few days back," Isaac informed him. "He don' git down with them white folks. He stayed down wit' the blacks. I know'd he wuz in trouble 'cause thet Indian come in leading a pack mule. He ain't never had no pack mule. He traded thet mule off to some pilgrims an' went to buy him some rum. But he don' drink much of it. He jest finds him a black gal an' stays shacked up wif her a day or so."

Isaac laughed. "You know, them Indians be jest lak them white mens. They learn right fast lak, thet black don' rub off."

Milton nodded his head in agreement. Then he asked, "He ride east?"

"Yes, suh, right on toward the Anglo settlements over at the bayou," said Isaac, pointing east, "on the Old San Antonio Road."

Milton lifted a hand in parting.

"So long. Has a nice trip," Isaac called after him.

Milton rode out onto the Old San Antonio Road. He rode facing the direction of the new-rising sun.

There was no traffic before daylight and only a small amount during the day. The road was quagmire from tree line to tree line. No wagons or buggies had been traveling this road. The trip by packtrain took a good two weeks or more to travel the one hundred and fifteen miles between Nacogdoches, Texas, and its sister city Natchitoches, Louisiana, during the rainy season. A light buggy and wagon traveled only during a dry part of the year.

Because of the thick undergrowth, a rider could not pass through the forest and get any relief from the muddy road. A trip on the roads of East Texas was a venture into madness during the spring.

Milton met two riders and one packtrain the entire day.

It was not until morning of the second day that he reached the Ayish Bayou settlements, the distance of about thirty-eight miles from Nacogdoches. It had been a couple of years since he had been this far east.

The Ayish Bayou settlement was not a full-fledged community or town. It was just what it was called, a settlement. There were a few businesses in the settlement, but none centrally located. These businesses included sawmills, gristmills, inns, carpenters, mercantiles, and other businesses to make the settlement self-supporting.

The Spanish established Mission Nuestra Señora de los Dolores de los Ais to serve the Ais Indians around 1717. The French in the area caused it to be short lived and it was abandoned. It was reestablished off and on for the next fifty years.

In the past few years the area had been losing its Mexican influence with the influx of Anglo settlers and border jumpers. The Mexican government had established the settlement as a political department, but the citizens still had not established a town.

Milton rode into the settlement and found Almanzon Houston's Inn. Milton dismounted, walked to a puddle of water, and cleaned the mud off his moccasins before going into the inn.

"Hey, mister, you tryin' to spoil it fer the rest of us?" a man on the porch asked.

"Clean feller, ain't he?" another remarked.

"Ole Houston see him an' he'll be wantin' all of us to clean our feet," the first one complained.

"My wife already got me broke," a third man on the other end of the porch informed any who were listening.

"You know, my daddy said he talked to a seaman that'ud been to an island called Nippon. He tole Paw them folks took off their shoes every time 'afore they went into their house," the second man said.

"Is thet a fact?"

"So he tole Paw."

"Hey, mister, you ever been to thet place called Nippon?" one of the men asked Milton.

Milton didn't answer, but passed on into the inn. He moved to a table that would leave his back to the wall and he could observe all comings and goings. He placed his long rifle on pegs on the wall behind him, sat down, and waited.

A man got up from a table where he had been talking with some of the customers. He walked over to Milton's table.

"How do, mister? What be the fair?" asked Almanzon Houston. The lingo was frontier, the accent New York.

"Breakfast. Plenty of coffee," ordered Milton.

Houston gave Milton's order to a black serving girl and returned to his table. The men's conversation was Houston's favorite, politics. He had finished his job as innkeeper for now, except for taking the money.

Breakfast was cornbread, a large helping of cracked-corn mush, and venison steak. The steak was large enough for a hungry man. It seemed that if it were not for corn, most Anglo Texans would go hungry most of the time.

"Comin' or runnin' back?" an elderly man asked Milton, a dried-up wisp of a man over seventy years of age.

"Never run back to nowhere," Milton told him.

"A stayer, huh? You look the type thet wouldn't," the old man told him. His age let him be bold. "Big men think they don't never gotta run. Been some of the places I be, you'd think different."

Milton kept his peace.

"You look like a feller thet'd be lookin' for somethin' or somebody," said the Wisp.

"Yep."

"A man thet'd look things over real close like when he come into a room, an' then make sure his back is again' the wall, is either lookin' or runnin'," the Wisp observed. "Since you tole me you don't run, an' I believe you, then I reckon you gotta be lookin'."

Milton continued to eat. If the old man wanted something or was going to tell him something, he would get it said.

"Been sittin' in this settlement over three year now. Been watchin' folks come an' go. The good uns and the bad uns," the old man told Milton. "Maybe I seed who you be lookin' fer."

"I could be one of the bad uns," Milton told the Wisp.

"Nope. Can't be. Good uns don't run. Bad uns do," the Wisp informed Milton. "Maybe I seed this man. Course, with the Neutral so close, you gotta watch what ya say 'bout some folks," said the Wisp. "Hell, I didn't git to be over seventy by talkin' too much."

"A breed Coushatta. Dark. Looks Mexican. He's more Indian acting than white. Speaks Spanish, no English. First finger missing on his right hand," Milton told him.

"You cut thet finger off?" asked the Wisp.

"Nope. He lost it in another fight some time ago," admitted Milton. "He does like to fight. Especially when he gets a gut full of rum."

"A bad un, huh?"

"He thinks so."

"Can't trust them damn breeds. They's worse than a blood. I know. I could spot one of them breed heatherns as far as I could see him," the old man informed Milton.

Milton remained silent.

"I seed the buck you be lookin' fer," said the Wisp.

Milton sat with his coffee, waiting for the old man to finish.

The old man was dying to tell him, but he wanted Milton to ask. "When?"

"He rode through here 'bout a week ago. Sorrel hoss. Mexican saddle. Thought he wuz tough. Acted tough. But I knowed he wuz a runner," said the Wisp. "He'll never stand man to man with nobody. He went on east, outta town. The Neutral, I reckon. That's where the rest of the trash is."

There was that good-over-evil business again. Milton knew that Thumping Turtle would stand nose to nose with anyone. He was a fighter, and a damned good one.

"Thanks," Milton told the old man.

"You gonna go where you have to go to git him?" asked the Wisp.

"Yep."

"Bet you do. Yep, you ain't no runner. Know'd thet when I first seed you," the old man told him.

Milton paid for his fare and told Houston to give the old man anything he wanted. Houston took out some money and waved as Milton passed outside. He went to his horse and tightened the cinch, then climbed aboard.

"Come back to see us, Clean Foot," one of the men on the porch called.

The Wisp followed Milton out onto the porch. He watched Milton ride out of town, remembering when he himself had once ridden to adventure. He bet the tall, dark man was not only a stayer, but he was a winner also.

Chapter Seven

The red quagmire dried up slightly during the day and made traveling easier. Then, late in the afternoon, it started raining hard and the wind blew sheets of water. The world was blotted out behind a wall of water and black clouds. Milton knew that he was in a storm danger zone.

He let the horse pick its way down the trail. There was no use in stopping. He and the animal would be just as miserable under a pine tree as out on the road. And trees were a magnet for lightning.

Milton looked up, squinting his eyes against the driving rain. Lightning cracked on all sides. A bolt exploded close enough that he could smell the burnt sulfur of its power. He was about to ask Great Thunder to keep his bolts of lightning to himself when he saw a dark cloud dip down to the ground. The roar was deafening. The whirling wind whipped leaves and tree branches around him. Ice balls fell from the sky, beating down upon his hat and stinging his arms and body. His horse reared and he fought for control.

The Devil Wind suddenly lifted the cloud like a woman tucking up her skirts for a run and the loud roar ceased just as quickly as it had come. The wind and clouds raced on, moving from eastward. It had come quickly and it had gone quickly.

If Milton had been a more religious man, and subject to displays of emotion, he would have fallen off his horse and given thanks to someone or something for sparing his life. As it was, he sat dumbfounded on his nervous horse. He felt his smallness. He had faced something he was powerless to fight.

That something was the power of the Great One Above. His grandfather had called Him Asgaya Galulati.

Milton had heard of these great Devil Winds, as the Texas Indians called them. He had seen their aftereffects. But this was the first time he had been so close to their breath. It was not a comfortable feeling.

After he had soothed the fear out of his horse, he rode on. He rode late, trying to get distance between himself and the Devil Wind that tossed trees around like a small boy tosses twigs.

He spent another night in a cold, fireless camp. The discomfort did not bother him overly much. He was a man of the woods. He had trained to be a Cherokee warrior as a boy. He had joined Andrew Jackson as a teenage boy to fight against the Creek Red Sticks, traditional enemies of the Cherokee. He knew about the discomforts of being a soldier, a frontiersman, and a man of the gun. Life was never easy for his sort. But it was a full, exciting life, as long as it lasted.

Morning found him on the road again, weaving in and out of bogs. He rode until he reached the Sabine River settlements. The settlements were a wide scattering of homes west of the river. The district of Sabine had been established in 1824 when Mexico had won its independence from Spain. Like the younger Ayish Bayou District, it was carved out of the district of Nacogdoches.

The Sabine settlement was like the Ayish Bayou in another respect, there being only a few Mexican settlers left. The Mexicans were not trusted and were kept out of local elected offices. It was quite a contrast from Nacogdoches, where the Spanish, and later Mexican, settlers allowed their new Anglo citizens full membership in community affairs.

Milton found no inn. But he did find the home of James Gaines, first alcalde of the district of Sabine. His house was not far from the Sabine River and the ferry that went by his name.

"How do? My name is James Gaines," the alcalde introduced himself.

"Hicks," was all Milton told him. He knew Gaines to be one of the local political leaders and part of what little law there was in the border area. "I come lookin' for a man."

"Who sent you, may I ask? Colonel Piedras or the alcalde?" asked Gaines.

"Neither. Bean," replied Milton.

"Must be after some Indian buck, then," ventured Gaines.

"A breed Coushatta named Thumping Turtle. Got drunk an' killed two men an' a woman," Milton informed him. "I aim to bring him back."

"Hell, if'n it's Indians killin' Indians, who gives a good goddamn?" Gaines growled.

"I give a damn anytime a man kills a woman," Milton informed him.

"She somebody you know?"

"Never laid eyes on the woman," Milton admitted.

"She be a white woman?" Gaines asked, not believing a man would go to all this trouble looking for an Indian who had killed an Indian woman.

"She was a Mexican settler's wife," Milton told him.

"Then what's the worrying? It ain't no difference to me if'n it be Mexican or Indian," said Gaines. "The more rid of 'em both, the more room for us God-fearin' white folks, is what I say."

Milton had noticed that the farther east he had come, the more Anglo it became. By the time he had gotten east of Ayish Bayou, all of the people he saw were Anglo. And they didn't care much for Mexico, Mexicans, or Indians. That was the reason the Mexican settlers in the area kept such a low profile. These Anglo people, even old settlers like Gaines, were still oriented toward the United States. But they had lived independently in isolation so long that they were mainly for themselves and to hell with the rest of the world.

"I be needing something to eat," Milton told Gaines.

"Down at the ferry. A man and woman has been runnin' my ferry the last couple of weeks. She feeds people passin' through," Gaines told him. "An' look, Hicks, once you cross the river on my ferry, you then be in the ole Neutral Strip. Nobody had jurisdiction over thet strip of land for years. It be a haven for all kinds of outlaws, from both Mexico an' America. The biggest part of 'em are American. But most of 'em don't know or give a damn thet the United States an' Mexico settled it up last year. The border of Texas is now the Sabine River. So once acrost the Sabine, you be in America."

"I'll remember that. Reckon there's American law I could find over there?" Milton asked.

Gaines laughed. "Not goddamned likely, mister. It'd take an army to clear thet bunch outta there. A lawman would be a fool to go in there. You best be careful yourself. Very careful. An' don't let 'em know you be Mexican law."

"Thanks, Mr. Gaines."

"Yes, sir, Mr. Hicks."

Gaines watched the tall man ride away. He couldn't figure out if the man was Anglo and Mexican, Anglo and Indian, or all three. Maybe he was one of them that called themselves Black Dutch. He did speak good English. Better than most folks Gaines knew. Whatever he was, he was a big one. And a damned fool for chasing anyone in the old Neutral Strip.

Then he remembered. The man must be that big Indian breed Bean and Austin was always using. He was reported to be a tough one. But Gaines wasn't sure he was tough enough to go into the Neutral and come out alive.

Milton rode to a small log cabin on the banks of the river. Two small boys and a girl played in the mud, making a small town with houses and streets. All three looked malnourished, and their bellies were swollen from intestinal parasites and worms. Their skin was blotched red from insect bites. All three looked as if they had had the swamp fever.

A bark roofed arbor stood beside the house. Split log tables and benches were the furniture. As he stepped from his saddle, a woman came outside. She was plain and her clothes were far from new. Her stringy blond hair fell below her drooping shoulders. He wondered why white frontier women always seemed so overworked, plain, and subdued of all emotion except disgust and anger at the world. These women married young, had children young, and so many it seemed as if they had them by the litter. They worked hard and usually died young. He reckoned that was reason enough to be angry at the world when a person came right down to it.

"What could I do for you, mister?" the woman asked, her thin, hard lips showing no sign of welcome.

"I would like something to eat," Milton told her.

"Got some bear meat, corn pone, beans, an' some greens fresh from the woods. Thet be okay?" she asked.

"Yes, ma'am. You cook it, I'll eat it," he informed her.

"The coffee was cooked earlier an' has water added to it," she explained.

"That'll be just fine," he assured her.

He sat on a bench and watched the children playing in the mud. He loved children.

The woman brought a tin cup of coffee first. He drank it, glad for its warmth even if it was diluted.

A man, looking as poorly kept and as used up as the woman, walked up. He did try to look pleasant. "Well, I didn't ferry you acrost, so you musta come in from the west."

Milton nodded his head. "Yes."

"Goin' to Natchitoches?" the man asked.

"Might." Milton swallowed some more of the diluted coffee.

The man looked closely at Milton. The tall, dark man looked like a man of the gun to him. He could either be hired out by the Mexican Government as a lawman, or he could be looking to settle a feud. The man wished a few times he were a man of the gun so he could settle a few feuds. Come to think of it, the tall man could be running from trouble. He doubted that.

"I be Nat Ellis."

"Milton Hicks." Milton didn't offer to shake hands.

"If you be after somebody, Mr. Hicks, maybe I could help you some," Nat offered. He figured Milton was a man of the law.

Milton sat a moment. Was he that obvious to this man, or was he just hoping to get in on a little excitement? Nat had been here at the ferry for a couple of weeks, so he might have seen Turtle. Nat was the type who would tell all he knew, just to make himself seem important. Or he could tell anyone what they wanted to hear, not knowing a thing about the subject, just to be part of the action. Milton had an idea Nat would only tell him what he knew. This man wanted to help because that was the only way he would ever be part of something exciting, and he had a chance to be on the winning side for a change.

"I'm looking for a breed Indian. Dark-skinned and big. He's ridin' a sorrel hoss with a Mexican saddle. Finger on right hand missing. Speaks Spanish, but little or no English," Milton told Nat.

"God yes, I seed that big bugger. Over a week ago. He wuz a mean sucker," Nat complained. "He smelt like a rum factory. He had two sacks acrost the back of his saddle. Reckon they wuz full of rum jugs. He et. Then he got drunk. He wouldn't pay for nothin', so's I tole him to leave. He got real mean an' started yellin' somethin'. A man wuz here thet spoke thet Spanish. He tolt me thet that Indian tole him he'd jest as soon kill wimmin an' kids as he would to drink rum."

The old scare tactics.

Nat continued. "He got in with two men from the Neutral Grounds. One wuz a Mexican and one was Anglo white trash. They cut up another man whilst they wuz here, took his money, an' made me carry 'em acrost the river. I ast for money, but thet dirty-mouthed Indian tole me something. The Mex with him told me the Indian said for me to go screw my mule. Mister Gaines took the pay outta my wages."

You're alive, thought Milton.

The man cursed and growled, "If I'ud had my rifle, I woulda kilt thet Injun. I'd kilt him shore as sin."

Mrs. Ellis brought Milton his food and he ate. She was a good cook. Now, if she were only clean.

He paid his bill and had Nat take him across the river.

"If'n you catch them three, put a bullet in 'em fer me!" called Nat.

Milton did not feel that needed answering. He didn't bother to raise his hand in the usual farewell.

Chapter Eight

Once Milton was across the river, he was in the United States of America, and what had once been called the Neutral Strip. The Neutral Strip was land between the Sabine River and the Arroyo Hondo. The Hondo was a tributary of the Red River, and was usually dry. This area became disputed land when the United States and Spain could not agree on a boundary line between the two countries. In 1806 the strip of land was declared uncontrolled by either country, and neither country would have legal jurisdiction.

In 1818 the question was supposedly settled between Spain and the United States with the Florida Purchase. In the Adams-Onís Treaty the two countries agreed to the Sabine River as the boundary and the United States in return would give up all future claims on Texas.

The Mexican revolution against Spain held up ratification of the treaty. Mexico gained its independence from Spain in 1824. Mexico agreed in principal with the treaty, but they did not sign the treaty until 1828.

During the years of dispute the Neutral Strip had become a haven for outlaws. No legal or moral laws could touch them. It meant little to them that the United States now had jurisdiction over their lives.

The road Milton traveled was still the Camino Real. It passed through Campti, a small trading post in the Neutral Strip, and on to Fort Jessup on the eastern edge of the Strip. A few miles east of Fort Jessup was Natchitoches, Louisiana, sister city to Nacogdoches, Texas. An old Indian legend told the story of how Natchitoches and Nacogdoches were established.

A chief the Caddo tribe had two strong-willed sons, one
named Natchitoches and the other Nacogdoches. Both wanted
to become chief of their people after the old father passed on.
The tribe was evenly divided in support of the two boys. To
keep peace among his people, the old chief decided that he
would split the two sons up. He sent one son to form a town
east of the Sabine River, and the other to form a town west of
the river. They were not to call themselves Caddo, but name
their tribes after themselves. Peace was kept among the people, and a military and economic bond was established between the two towns. That relationship was broken up by the
coming of the white man, and few, if any, members of the
Nacogdoches or Natchitoches tribes still existed.

Milton rode into the old trading post of Campti as the sun
reached its zenith.

The area around the post was crowded with pack animals
and their handlers. American soldiers searched for a dry spot
to sit and rest. Only the lieutenant in charge and an ensign
rode horses. There were about forty soldiers in all. Their mission was to give the packtrain protection until it cleared the
Neutral Strip. They did not have the mission of clearing the
Strip of bandits.

The largest packtrain belonged to Frost Thorn. One belonged to John Durst and another one to William Goyens.
Milton recognized the head drover of one pack train as belonging to an old warrior from Andrew Jackson's army, Captain
Stephen Prather. Prather had an Indian trading post near
Bevil's Diggings. He had been the one who led the Indians
into the Fredonians' camp near Nacogodoches during the Rebellion.

With the presence of the United States Army some law was,
by stages, coming into the Strip. Law would expand over the
Strip and outlaws be forced to vacate the area in search of
safer places. Milton knew many of them would come to Texas.

He made his way to the hitching post and tied his horse

after stepping down. The pony sighed and dropped a hip. The stud looked pitiful and dejected.

Milton smiled. This horse had character.

Soldiers came out of the trading post with an assortment of items, complaining about the high prices. They had learned one of the facts of life in the Neutral Strip. Everyone was out to get your money, one way or the other.

Milton stood away from everyone, waiting for the packtrain and soldiers to clear out. No one would come around as long as they were present. Time passed as it always did with him. With his stoic patience, it did just that, it passed. Two and a half hours passed before the packtrain, along with its military escort, left on its way to Natchitoches.

He went into the building. There was a rude table of food to his left. He cut off a large slice of cooked venison, and a large slice of dark bread that was for sale, and walked to the counter. "Beer," he ordered.

The man behind the counter dipped a partially clean mug into a barrel. After wiping the bottom off with a dirty rag, he sat it down on the counter.

Milton paid the man, picked up the mug, and walked outside. He sat down on a bench on the porch and watched two pigs root in the muddy road.

He didn't ask if Thumping Turtle had passed through. These people were not necessarily in league with the outlaws in the area, but they did as much as possible to keep a peaceful relationship with them. The outlaws also made it a point not to bother the people of Campti. It was the only trading post near them, so they did not wish to run them out.

"How do, mister?" a man on a bench on the other end of the porch greeted Milton.

"How do?" returned Milton, continuing to eat and drink.

"Reckon the States will ever tame the Neutral Strip?" the man asked Milton.

"Someday. But I wouldn't wait on it. It'll take some time," Milton assured him.

"I ain't seen you around before," the man commented.

"Nope."

Silence.

Joel Bartlett was not the kind of man to be easily intimidated, but there was something about this man that gave him pause. Some men you did not run head-on into. You took your time. This was one of those men.

Who was this guy? Joel asked himself. What was this guy?

No doubt he came from Texas. He rode a Plains Indian horse and had a Spanish saddle. The tall man was dark like a Spaniard, but he did not dress or talk like one. He dressed like an American frontiersman. He had waited for the packtrains and military escort to depart before he had come to the store.

"You be from Texas?" Joel asked.

"I be" was Milton's only comment.

"Business or pleasure?" he dared ask.

Milton looked at him steadily for a moment. Then he gave a clipped answer of "Both."

Silence again.

It was suddenly broken by the crack of a rifle from across the road. The rifleman was hidden by brush and trees.

The beer mug was nearly to Milton's lips when the shot rang out. The almost empty mug fell to the floor and Milton readied himself for battle.

Milton heard a gasp to his right and the man who had "Howdied" him staggered off the porch and fell to the ground.

The storekeeper ran out to the porch. He had no weapon.

Three men came around from the back of the building. People stuck their heads out the doors of a few small shacks, but none came outside.

Milton walked over to join the crowd around the fallen man.

"Who do you reckon he be?" asked one of the men.

"Somebody with a powerful mad enemy," said another.

"Yeah, one that is a good shot," said the storekeeper.

"I seed him 'round a couple times before. He don't do nothin' but stand around," said the first man.

"Hell, thet sounds about like the rest of us. I don't want to git shot fer jest stan'in' around," the second man told them.

Laughter.

"Is he dead?" asked the storekeeper.

"Dead'ern a roasted 'possum."

"If'n he's dead, we might as well fin' out who he be," the first man told them.

"Not who he be, who he wuz."

The men rolled Joel face up. The storekeeper went through his pockets.

"Here's something," the storekeeper said. He unfolded the paper he found. "It's a U.S. marshal's commission. Bet he's out of Fort Jessup."

"Wal, he's outta this world right now."

More laughter.

"Ain't thet a fact."

"Name of Joel Bartlett," the storekeeper told them.

"Wal, now, not only was his name Joel Bartlett, ole Stand Around was dumb as hell."

"He had to be dumb to come in here as a lawman," the third man growled.

"Yeah, somebody shore done us a favor," the first man commented.

The men looked at each other. Then they looked at Milton.

Milton went back to his meat and bread. After he had finished, he went back to his waiting place under a pine tree. It was away from people and the action going on.

The men in front of the store were not concerned about a U.S. marshal being killed in their midst. Any lawman would be a fool to come out here alone.

That brought up a question. Who was that tall dark man over there? They looked at Milton with suspicion, but no one approached him.

Milton could easily have tracked the assassin down, but he

did not want to go on any wild chase through the bush of the
Neutral Strip. He would wait for an opportunity to find someone to guide him directly to what he was looking for.

This strip of land was one hell of a place, especially for a
man of the law, he observed.

Milton continued to wait.

Chapter Nine

Two men rode out of the forest from the south. The trail was so narrow that they were forced to ride single file. Both men were Anglos dressed in frontier garb.

One look at the rifle the lead man carried convinced Milton that the two men were Neutral Strip outlaws. He could tell from the peculiar appearance of the rifle's action that the man was carrying an American Hall breach-loading flintlock. He had only seen one, but he knew what it was. This trash could not afford to buy such a weapon and it had to be stolen.

Milton watched them go into the trading post. After they had disappeared inside the building, he got on his horse and rode down the same trail the men had ridden in on. He rode for over three miles before he found a suitable clearing to turn his horse around in. He sat on one side of the trail and waited.

The forest had quieted with his entrance. He sat in silence and waited. The trees and brush closed in on all sides. He could not see the sky above him, or see the stream gurgling off to his left.

When his animal brothers of the forest realized that he was no threat to them, they returned to their normal activities. A squirrel, called *saloli* by the Cherokee, barked to its mate. Milton could hear the footsteps of a family of deer, called *awi*, with a newborn one tripping along. A skunk, called *dili*, crossed the trail near by, pausing long enough to stare at these two strange creatures. He did not care for the smell of the horse, turned up his nose, and departed.

Milton stepped down from his horse to wait. It was a long wait.

Suddenly the forest gave a startled chatter to the north, then quieted. The silence moved from the north to the south in his direction. His brothers of the animal world had signaled him that strangers were coming.

Milton stepped back upon his horse. He cocked his rifle.

The two men stopped when he kicked his horse out onto the narrow trail, blocking their passage. They were the two men he had seen at the trading post.

"Hold with the rifle, mister. And you in the rear, take care. I will shoot through your friend to kill you," Milton warned.

The two men froze, afraid their horses might move and get them into trouble.

The lead man had the pleasure of looking down the barrel of an .80-caliber Kentucky rifle. The hole in the end of the barrel appeared to the lead man to be as large as a rain barrel.

"Hold on there, mister! We ain't got no money," the lead man told him.

Calling everyone "mister" was big on the frontier.

"Who is it, Eb? What the hell is goin' on?" asked the man in the rear.

"Shut up, Reed. We got trouble here," barked Eb.

The three of them sat and waited. Milton was in no hurry. He knew their type always was. Hurrying men make mistakes, some fatal.

"What you want, mister?" asked Eb. "You be the law?"

"What'n the gawddamned hell do he want, Eb?" demanded Reed.

"Gawddammit! Hush to hell up, Reed! Can't you see we got serious trouble here?" demanded Eb.

"Hell, Eb, I can't see a gawddamned thing!" spat Reed.

"If'n you could come up here, gawddammit, I'd sure as hell let you be the one lookin' down the hole of this eighty," Eb snapped.

"That's a big un all right," agreed Reed. "He a big un, Eb?"

"He shore ain't no dwarf. Not an' shoot thet thing!" Eb informed Reed.

Milton waited for the two men to settle down. It was evident that they had been sampling the store's rum.

"You're blockin' the trail, mister," Eb told Milton. He tried to make it polite. Politeness came before bravery when you are looking down the tube of death with the killer at the other end.

"I'm lookin' for somebody," Milton informed them.

"We don't know nobody," Reed said from his position in the rear.

"Gawddammit, Reed, stop bein' so gawddamn brave back there! You ain't lookin' down the barrel of this cannon!" complained Eb. Then he told Milton, "Now look, mister, we ain't seed nobody. Nobody at all. We jest got here. Ain't be here long."

"What's back down the trail behind me? An' don't tell me you don't know, boys," Milton ordered, "—you came from that direction a while ago."

"He kin go plum to hell, Eb," said Reed.

"Gawddammit, Reed, would you shut up!" yelled Eb. Desperation had entered his voice. This big man in front of him was unsettling. "Now look, mister, we don't know nobody around here."

"I'm gettin' tired of holding this thing," Milton told him.

"Wal, there's a family of them funny Frenchies, I think they's what you call them French Canadians. Jest a ways down the trail. They got them a place right smack dab out in the middle of nowhere on the edge of the swamp," Eb informed him.

"What's down past them?" asked Milton.

"Camps," Eb told him, his eyes still on the rifle Milton was holding.

"You two see a breed from Texas called Thumping Turtle?" asked Milton.

"We ain't tellin' ya nothin', right, Eb?" spat Reed.

"Reed, I shore do wisht to hell you wuz up here an' I wuz back there," groaned Eb.

"Damn! There's two of us, Eb!" Reed reminded him.

"Yeah, with me in front," complained Eb.

"Do you two talk all the time?" an exasperated Milton asked.

"When there ain't no wimmin," said Eb.

"Or booze," put in Reed from the back.

"An' I ain't half scart to death," admitted Eb.

"Hell, I ain't sceered a nobody," Reed burst out.

"An', gawddammit, you ain't in front!" a worried Eb informed Reed.

"I asked a question. I mean to get an answer," Milton told them. The tone said, *And I ain't waiting much longer for an answer.*

Eb looked at the long Kentucky rifle. He was beginning to sober up. That thing was wicked, but the tall man holding it was even worse. He unconsciously cleared his throat. "We may a seed him."

"I'm waitin'," barked Milton.

"Hell, mister, we don't keep track of the comin's and goin's of everybody we've seed!" complained Eb.

Milton knew he was not going to get much out of these two. Code of the outlaw. Don't tell on anyone to an outsider. He sat his horse, unmoving. At least he knew there was a small group of Acadians down the trail. The outlaw gangs were probably holed up for better weather. Most all packtrains and travelers moved under military escort. But some didn't.

Milton automatically loosened his tomahawk before he backed his pony into the small clearing. He ordered, "Pass on ahead of me."

Eb started forward.

"Duck, Eb!" screamed Reed, raising his rifle to fire.

Milton was faster and the huge rifle ball smashed into Reed's face, taking most of his brains out as it passed through and out the back of his head. The sound of the explosion was deafening in the close area.

Before Eb could react with the American Hall, Milton

pulled and let fly with his tomahawk. It flew straight and true, cutting through Eb's left arm and sticking into his chest. The rifle slipped out of his hands and slid to the ground.

"Reed, you wuz always a dumb-ass," were the last words Eb said as he followed his rifle to the ground, his left arm still pinned to his chest.

The three horses stood still, throwing their heads in excitement, but not bolting. These animals were trained to operate under the gun.

Milton stepped to the ground. He walked over to where Eb lay and pulled the tomahawk from his chest. With a swift blow he sunk his tomahawk deep into Eb's skull. Milton had seen too many dead men on the battlefield rise up and kill. He moved to Reed and quickly dispatched him, necessary or not.

Milton did not take scalps as most red men and white frontiersmen did. He didn't think one way or the other about it's being proper. He just didn't do it himself—one of his personal idiosyncrasies. But he did something that was strange and made most men uncomfortable. He went to every dead man and looked him in the face for a long moment. Not to every dead man he saw, just those he killed.

He picked up the Hall and tied it to Eb's saddle. Then he lifted Eb and laid him across the saddle of his horse. He pulled Eb's horse into the clearing and did the same thing with Reed. With Reed's horse's reins tied to Eb's horse's tail, he turned his horse around and moved south down the trail.

Killing these two men didn't stir Milton Hicks's emotions. He had seen many more deaths than he had seen birthings. He had killed more than most men had seen buried. Fighting and killing, loving and hating, living and dying, were all part of his world. He accepted one as easily and as naturally as he did any other. This was his training; this was his way.

Milton rode, his eyes and nose on extra alert to compensate for the temporary loss of hearing from the rifle blast.

The trail skirted the marsh and followed it until it reached the edge of a clearing. The clearing was located near what he would call more of a bayou than a swamp. It had been cleared and used for a number of years.

Three log houses, one larger than the others, and four smaller outbuildings stood on high ground in the clearing. It was a small family community huddled together against the outer world.

A little garden, freshly turned and planted, lay in the only spot cleared of enough trees to allow the sun to shine through. A pigpen was fenced on the east side of the clearing. The pen was used to hold hogs being fattened; the rest ran wild. A small pen with two old broken-down horses was not far from one of the houses. The outlaws would not allow them to keep stock of any worth.

Milton was alerted by his keen sixth sense. He started to cock his rifle, but then relaxed. He was nailed and nailed good. He could feel the presence of the man.

Chapter Ten

"*Grand homme,* you move the one toe, I put you down from the horsey, me," a man's voice told him from his left. "*Parlez-vous Français?*"

"Some French, but not what you speak. I read some French," Milton informed him.

Milton didn't fear this man might shoot him. He would already have pulled the trigger if that had been his intention.

"Oh? You no *parlez?* Some trouble we got, eh? My *anglais,* he is no so good. I don' read no *français,* me. But I tank maybe you understand, put zee gun down, you."

Milton had no trouble understanding that part. He let his rifle slide to the ground, butt first, then pushed it so the brush broke its fall. He had carried that long rifle for fifteen years and it was a part of him.

"Now, *mon homme,* zee pistol an' zee *couteau* of de Bowie, . . . ah, zee Bowie knife, let zay all slide down at zee same time, *oui?* All of she be next, eh?"

Milton aimed the pistol for the heavy brush and flipped the knife at the same time. It darted forth and stuck in a tree next to the man's head.

The man automatically ducked from normal reaction. He was not the killer type, for he did not squeeze the trigger.

Milton pulled his tomahawk and threw it in one fluid motion that comes from years of practice. The tomahawk struck the outside of the man's right shoulder, slicing off the flesh to the bone. The blade of the tomahawk passed through the heavy cloth of the shirt and pinned him to the trunk of a tree.

The man dropped his rifle and it went off as it hit the

ground. He yelped in surprised pain, "Oooooyyyyyeeeeee! Oh, *grand homme*, you 'ave made me dead already, me!"

Milton stepped to the ground and picked up his rifle, knife, and pistol, leaving the man hanging there.

The man braced his legs and leaned limply against the tree, not knowing yet if he was on his way to the dead or would remain with the living.

Milton quickly looked toward the buildings in the clearing. People came out of the houses to look in the direction the noise had come from.

He picked up the man's discharged rifle. With a powerful pull he jerked the tomahawk loose from the cypress tree. His favorite weapon had tasted blood twice today.

The Frenchman sagged a moment, then stood upright, leaning against the tree for support.

"You don' kill me, eh, no?" the Frenchman asked.

"You'd already be dead if'n I was in the killin' mood," Milton informed him. Then he ordered, "Tell your people to stay back and put down all weapons. All people will come out of the houses, women, children, all."

"You no kill wimmin an' babies? No, you cannot!" the man pleaded.

"I ain't in the habit of killin' women and babies."

The man looked at Milton, wanting to believe. He had no choice but to believe. He yelled out commands in his strange French dialect.

A man, two women, and six children joined the others in the yard. An older woman took all of the weapons from the men and carried them to the edge of the clearing. She deposited them beside the trail and walked back to the group. The weapons all were old French-made rifles of early- and mid-1700 vintage. The rifles and shotguns were all of a small-game bore. There was an assortment of knives and a short sword.

Milton motioned the wounded man out onto the trail. He led Milton to the clearing. As they passed the stack of weapons, Milton added the wounded man's rifle to the pile.

Two women raced forward to the wounded man. They ripped his shirt off. One of the women nearly swooned when she saw the large chunk of flesh cut from his shoulder. The wound was bleeding profusely.

"Fix him," Milton ordered.

"How?" The question came from the daughter, but it could have come from all of them.

"He bleeds. A hot iron," Milton told them.

When it was understood by all, negative cries went up.

From all except the old man, the papa. He said, *"Oui, oui,* it is good, it be, yes."

The old woman went into the house after he had given instructions. Shortly, thick smoke rose from the chimney.

They sat the wounded man beside the house and leaned him up against the wall. They made him as comfortable as possible, then waited.

The door opened and the old woman came out of the house with a hot iron used for pressing clothes. The iron was so hot the rags she had around the handle were smoking. She handed the hot iron to the old man.

All of them made a sign of the cross.

Without hesitation or a word the old man walked over to the wounded man and slapped the hot iron against the wound. The flesh sizzled and sent out a stench of burnt flesh and blood.

The wounded man screamed and jumped straight up. He fell back against the wall of the building in a dead faint. He slowly slipped down the wall until he was in a sitting position on the ground. The bleeding had stopped but he would have the mark of a flatiron on his shoulder for the rest of his life.

The younger men picked up the unconscious man and placed him on an outdoor table. The man's wife moaned and whimpered as if she were also hurting. The daughter flashed Milton a hard look full of hate.

He would have to watch this teenage girl. He saw it in her eyes. She would kill him if she got the chance.

The older man came forward. "Me, Pepin Colbert, me. My family, zay be here."

Milton nodded.

"Why do you come here, my *maision*, you? Why you hurt my boy, huh?" Pepin asked.

"I hurt your boy because he had a rifle on me," Milton replied. "I am here 'cause I'm look for a man."

"You fin' two already, eh? Why you need more?" Pepin asked, looking at the two men tied to their saddles.

"I don't find who I want. I still look," Milton told him. "Do you know these two men?"

Pepin walked to them and pulled their heads up by their bloody hair. After a look he said, "*Oui*, I know deez two *hommes, oui*. Zay be zee Neutral—how you say—Neutral Terrain, *oui*, Neutral Terrain *bors-la-loi*. Zee man outside zee law."

"You people are not?" demanded Milton.

"Oh, but no! We zee French Acadians, we. All of us, we. We come here long time. Terrain, he change, many times. Be France, be Spanish, be America. We do no change, we, no. We do not know who terrain she belong, but we change, no. We Acadians. We belong to us, we," Pepin assured Milton. "Dees *hommes* out of zee law, they come. Zay give we Acadians we all trouble, yes. Yes, you better know I speak true."

Milton understood their problem.

"You is zee law?" Pepin asked.

"Just for a short time. Only until I get my man," Milton told him. He didn't bother to tell Pepin he was Texas law.

"Dis be no good place for a man of zee law. Dis be no good place for nobody but zee Acadians. If zee outside-zee-law *hommes* keep comin' here, it be no good for we someday," complained Pepin.

"Are there more coming?" asked Milton.

"No, she not so many for a time now. For while, they be no increase. But they be too many big here now!" said Pepin.

"The Neutral Strip is part of the United States now," Milton informed them. "The Neches River is now the legal border of the U.S. and Mexico. More and more law will come to this part of Louisiana."

Pepin shrugged his shoulders as if the information meant little or nothing to him. He knew he would be dead and gone before law and order ever reached this far into the Strip.

It was late and the day was turning to dusk.

"I'll have to camp here for the night," Milton told them.

"You stay. Camp more near here, my *maison*. *C'est à votre disposition.* But no too close to water be, no, eh? Serpent, zee water thing, all over at night. Maybe you catcha zee alligator dis night, *oui?* She no be so funny to catch, monsieur," Pepin assured him with a laugh. "We take care of zee dead now."

Milton nodded that it should be done.

"No to worry, you, for bein' thees *hommes* dead. God, He don' care you kill thees kind of *homme*," Pepin told Milton.

Milton didn't stop to contemplate that. He had been at it too long and was past worrying about it. And, he had not been raised to worry about the religious implications of killing.

He returned to the pile of weapons and placed them near his camping place for the night. He made sure each weapon was unloaded. It would take the best gunman more than a minute to load any of the old guns.

The family returned to their individual chores, the women preparing the evening meal. The men took care of the two dead outlaws.

Rosemarie, Pepin's youngest daughter, brought Milton dry firewood. She returned a short time later with a request from her father for him to join the family for supper.

Milton checked the exact location of each weapon. Then he went to join the Colberts at their outside table.

The wounded member of the family sat in a chair by the table. Only the male members of the family were seated at the table.

"Zee hurt *homme* is my son, he, Richard," Pepin informed Milton.

"Oooowwwweee, monsieur, you nearly miss, but you hit my arm, you," Richard complained.

"I didn't miss," Milton told him.

"You aim to hit zee shoulder?" asked Richard, interest on his face.

"If I'd been aiming to kill you, you would be laid out with the other two," Milton informed him matter-of-factly.

"Zee one *homme* wit zee bad cut, she be dead wit zee hatchet, him?" asked Pepin.

"He be," said Milton.

"Aaaaaaeeeeiiii!" exclaimed Philippe Fave, the son-in-law.

"You don' kill my son, Richard, you, eh?" Pepin said it in a grateful manner.

The meal consisted of fish, the Acadians' main diet, greens from the forest, and early vegetables from the garden. The women were good cooks, even though most of the fare was fattening.

After the men finished their meal, they went to one side to talk while the women and children ate. When they had finished, they all joined in for dessert.

Milton approached them for some information. "I'm lookin' for a man. A breed Coushatta Indian named Thumping Turtle. Has he been around?"

The family members looked at each other. There was no doubt from their expressions that he had passed through. Thumping Turtle was making the rounds and leaving a trail. Milton was having no trouble following this man.

"*Oui*, we see dis *homme*, we," Pepin told Milton. "He be one bad Indian, thet one, yes. He done raped our babie, Rosemarie."

"He coulda askt." Rosemarie pouted.

I bet it was some rape, Milton thought. He lit up his clay pipe, offering the men tobacco.

The mother spewed a barrage of French.

"Mama, she say, you fin' that Indian, use your ax," said Pepin with a grin. "I theenk Mama, she be very angry."

"If I have to, I will," assured Milton.

"We no be outside of zee *loi*, zee law, as you say. We live here many year. All me, Mama's babies, be born here, he," Pepin informed Milton. "I be born Canada, me. Me mama, me papa brunged me here when I be leetle boy. It be one helluva hard time, you better believe it. Whew! But we French from Acadia. We do anything. Zen come America, outside-zee-law *homme*. Zay done be very bad. Take what zay want from we, zee Acadian. We no be enough Acadian to stop zees *hommes* from take what zay want, we. Zay tole we zis be Neutral Terrain, yes. How can zis be? We here. We no be neutral. We be inside zee law. But nobody has help us, we. So we do best we can, huh? We survive!"

Milton nodded his head. He had grown up in that situation in Tennessee.

"I understand. I ain't after all of them outlaws, but I am after this one. I'll catch him," Milton told them.

Milton didn't have legal authority, but he did have a mad on and a gun. If Bean accidentally died, his legal authority might be in doubt in Texas, since his was a verbal commission. But who in the hell would worry about his legal representation of the law in the old Neutral Strip? A man with a legal commission died just as easily as one without. That had been proven back in Campti.

After a short talk he returned to his camp.

It was still and damp at the edge of the bayou. There was a strong smell of rotten wood and rotting vegetation. He was glad that the heat of summer had not yet arrived. It would be a natural steambath in this area.

He made a careful search through his bedroll for any unwanted swamp guests.

The Colbert family remained outside until late that night. It was clear and no rain was in the air. The old man played an ancient concertina. The family members took turns singing sad, lonely songs about the plight of the Acadians. Their voices were full of sadness and emotion.

After everyone had gotten into the mood of music, Mama Colbert got out her fiddle to join her husband. The songs alternated between the happy, snappy dance tunes of fun to the sad wails of a people pushed back from civilization and forgotten. These were a strange people to Milton Hicks.

Chapter Eleven

The noise of movement woke him. He lay listening to the silence. Most of the animals and insects had quieted down for the night.

Milton's muscles tightened. He did not know who it was, but he was ready.

"Monsieur?" It was a female's voice. Rosemarie!

He sat up. He was thankful that most of the mosquitoes had bedded down for the night or at least taken a break. His face was already covered with bumps on top of bumps. He had used Spanish moss to make smoke to keep the mosquitoes at bay, but these Louisiana critters were a tough breed.

"It is I, Rosemarie. I want to make sure you know me is me. Zee ax, she be very accurate," Rosemarie told him.

"Your mama and papa know you're out here?" Milton demanded. He knew they did not know.

"Well, they no know me be here. But it no *difference* to make," she informed him.

"It damned sure will make a difference to me if Mama and Papa thinks I also raped their baby daughter," replied Milton. That was all he needed to add to his problems, to have a story going around that he, Milton Hicks, was a rapist.

She wished to lay another problem on him. "You take me you go, no?"

Without hesitation he gave her a firm "You're right, young lady, it's a no!"

"But, me, I like see that Thumpin' Turtle man again," she told him.

"After he raped you?" Milton grinned in the dark.

"What's a leetle rape?" she asked. "He ask me, I give it to him, me. He big man. He big all over!"

"Why do Mama and Papa think he raped you?"

"He no take me. I tole a him, 'You no take, I scream.' He no take, I scream. Loud," she informed him.

"Gawddamn!" he mumbled. "Look, I can't take you with me. Why don't you get married or something. Do something a girl oughta do."

"This girl oughta fin' Turtle," she insisted.

"I ain't takin' you with me." He might be in a fix with this screwy young woman.

"I can't marry nobody I meet yet. They no can make it with me," she complained. "They all leetle boys. Turtle, he be first man that do it right, by me. I follow him, me, you bet."

Oh, God! Milton told her, "I can't take you with me."

"I must go, me. I help Turtle. You bet I could help him. He no go *prison,* " she informed Milton.

She was as bold as brass. She wanted him to help her get to Turtle so she could help Turtle break away from him. Crazy! But he was beginning to think the whole Strip was a little on the crazy side.

He was quiet. What else could he say? What in the hell was she going to do?

"You no talk me?" Rosemarie complained.

"I done talked."

"You don't take me?" she demanded.

She was about to give him problems.

"Look. You can't go with me. I'm after a man the law wants. I must travel fast and with caution. How long do you think we'd last with you along? If we got to Thumping Turtle, we would still have to get out of this area. You would, in all probability, get him killed along with me," Milton told her.

"I need him, me! I need," Rosemarie groaned.

"Maybe when I get back to Texas and I find him, I'll send for you," Milton assured her.

"My family, she don't let me go to Texas," she complained.

"Then wait for him to settle up with the law for his crimes and he can come back here," explained Milton.

With his crimes, I'm cutting it short, thought Milton. No Indian, not even if he was a breed, was going to get by with killing three Spanish-speaking people. That was one of those times even Anglos considered Mexicans white.

She was silent, and it worried him. What if she started screaming, *"Rape!"* or making a fuss some other way? He knew he had only one recourse in that case: get on his horse and ride like hell.

Finally she said, "No, he will no never come back here. I think maybe you will kill him."

That's strictly up to him. He said out loud, "I can't take you."

"I be nice to you, me, you know? I come to you bed. You forget all the other women, I bet you much. You, me, go to bed, you no gonna be sorry you do that," she assured him.

Damn! What did this girl want? Was she trying to use him just to get to Turtle and pay him back for not taking her with him? Maybe she was trying to use him to get to Turtle to do a little cutting for revenge. Now, that was something he understood, revenge!

And he could not take her to his blankets. It was not because she was young. A girl should get a young start. It was not because he did not want to. He seldom turned down women he thought would be good. He would not take her to his blankets because of the circumstances. A man on the hunt or warpath had no place for romance. Besides, he needed the sleep.

"Look. There ain't no way I could get through those outlaw camps with you along. I ain't gonna try," he told her. *Damn little hot female*, he thought with a mental growl. "Stay home like a good girl. Marry some good Acadian boy an' have babies."

"I want to go with you," she insisted.

"I've got a long way to go. I'm going to do it alone," he told her, getting an edge of impatience in his voice. "So why don't you go back to the house? Don't cause any trouble, Rosemarie.

You know what would happen if your papa thought you was in trouble. He'd come out fightin' mad. So would the rest of your family. I would have to fight for my life an' there'd be a lot of killin'. I am a man of the gun, so you know who would get hurt the most. You wouldn't want that to happen, would you?"

Predict calamity and then appeal for sympathy and reason. Leave it to her to be the gracious one. And let her know that by her self-sacrifice, she saves them all. Who said old Milton Hicks had no idea what makes women tick?

"You think Papa an' the others, they come for me if trouble be me? For their Rosemarie?" she asked.

"You know them better than I do," he told her. *This just may work!*

"You be right. They come, you shoot. They come to rescue me, keep my virginity. You got all the guns." She sighed.

These white women were sure up on this virgin business. If they were not virgin, then they wanted everyone to believe they were.

She stood up. "Maybe I come to Texas. I come, fin' you, yes? I make you forget Mexican and Indian womans," she promised.

With that, she left.

Milton followed her with his ears. She went directly to her house and entered by the back way.

He shook his head with a sigh of relief. Arguing with a gun or knife was a lot more dangerous, but it was sure easier.

Chapter Twelve

Daylight came in the misty world of the swamp and bayou country. Milton came awake early as he always did. The newborn sun would not greet him on this day. It could not get through the fog and foliage around him.

He went to the bayou and took his morning dip. Rosemarie sat on a fallen log and watched him.

He packed his gear, saddled his horse, and was ready to ride at a moment's notice. He left his horse and equipment at the camp and stopped by the woodshed for an armload of wood. He carried it to Mama Colbert's outside cookstove.

Mama Colbert was already cooking the morning breakfast when Milton arrived. Without a word she poured him a cup of eye-opener coffee. And eye-opener it was, chicory leaves and all. It left his taste buds numb for the rest of the morning. Mama smiled when she saw his expression.

Pepin greeted him with a friendliness that Milton would not have expected. Both he and Mama Colbert had greeted him in a better manner this morning. Evidently they had considered things and felt it was by the grace of God and Milton Hicks that their son was still alive.

Rosemarie passed by, smiling at Milton to let him know that she liked what she had seen that morning.

"I hear that you Acadians have been here for a good while now," said Milton.

"*Oui.* Zee British, zay come to Canada, zay run us Frenchman's people outta Canada in seventeen an' seventy-five. It was that time you American's people call zee Frenchies and Indians War. We be in what ees now zee Nova Scotia.

Now was den called by us, Acadia. It be called thet for us over one hundred and seventy year, *oui*. Den come zee British. Zay don' ask us we go. Zay make we go, *oui*," Pepin told him. He gulped down the hot coffee and filled his cup with more. "Over three thousand Acadian who be we Frenchmans, we go. Leave all, homes, horses, chickens, all. British take all we do have then. Don' pay we, no. Jest say, you Frenchmans, don' belong here, no. So we go. I be twelve year old den. We be sent here in dis Louisiana land. We be in Acadia never more. Oh, we do had it bad. Whew! It be ver-ry bad, *oui*. Nobody want dis water Louisiana land. But we Acadian people, we do. We take it. We hold it."

"You Frenchmen did it to the Indians and then other white men did it to you," Milton informed Pepin.

"Oh, *oui, oui*, I do know dis. I no blame them red *homme* one little bit for mad he, no, sir, me. I know now why day red *hommes* fight so big for their homeland. You better believe me, yes. I gonna fight for dis land, me."

"I hope you and your family don't ever have to fight nobody. Maybe them outlaws will be driven out in a few years," Milton said, trying to give him hope. He knew what war did to the families caught in the middle of hostilities.

"I hope you do be right, mister tall *monsieur*. I hope you do be right," sighed Pepin. He was too old to start a new life if he should be driven out. He only hoped that the United States government would allow all the Acadians to remain on their own land in Louisiana.

Milton and Pepin had eaten by the time the rest of the family began to stir.

"Rest of zee family, much lazybones," Pepin told him. He and Mama were early risers.

The other members of the family were also generous with their greetings. All except the young Claudette. She had not forgiven him for the injury he had done her father. She had no concern with the circumstances, only hate for the perpetrator.

While the rest of the family ate, Milton tightened his saddle cinch and loaded his few belonging on the back of his saddle. He led his horse around to the front of the house. He held the rifles of the two outlaws in his hands.

The family came to the trail's edge where he stood.

"Pepin, you keep the two horses. They are in payment for the burial of those two," said Milton. He did not include payment for their hospitality to him. That would be an insult to these proud people.

"*Merci, grand homme!*" replied the surprised Pepin. He was not used to a fair shake from these Americans, let alone a gift from one of them. "Looky me, *grand homme*, I tole a you. Maybe eight or ten miles they be if down the trail you go, south. Zay be there one *grand camp des hors-la-loi*. You be careful, huh? She no be good place to be for such as you, eh?"

"I'll remember that," Milton replied. He turned to Richard and held out the American Hall. "A man who must defend an' feed his family needs a good rifle."

Richard stood without words to express his thanks. The pain in his arm was forgotten for the moment.

"*Grand homme*, I will say, *je vous remercie* for my broke-jaw *beau-frère*," laughed Philippe.

Milton handed Philippe the Charleville, the French-made model 1763 flintlock that had belonged to the second outlaw. The rifle was in excellent condition. "I suggest you hide both rifles along with the horses when not in use."

"*Entendu,*" they all agreed.

It was Philippe's turn to be "broke-jaw."

Milton glanced at Claudette. She was still not impressed by his show of friendship.

Without another word he got onto his pony and rode off.

Claudette screamed and jerked the rifle out of her father's hands. Richard tried to stop her, but the girl was too quick. She raised the rifle and tried to shoot Milton with it, but it was not loaded. She ran to the woodpile and picked up the ax. She was headed off by some of the boys in the family and her

Uncle Philippe. Claudette screamed and begged them to let her go.

Milton figured he had seen the Colbert family for the last time.

The longer Milton rode, the deeper he got into the swamp and rain forest bordering Louisiana and Texas. Most of the land was unchartered and untraveled by the outside world. Only the hardy Acadians traveled the waterways in their small flat-bottomed boats. It was only these displaced Frenchmen who were comfortable in this damp, insect-and-reptile infested waterland. The outlaws were here only out of necessity and would make no lasting impact upon the land.

Milton rode with caution. He was in hostile territory infested by another kind of snake. This kind killed not to defend, but because it could.

Other small trails crossed or ran into the main trail he was traveling. The trails had once been used only by animals. Now they were beaten out by men on the run.

The moss-covered trees with their new leaves of spring blotted out the sun. The smell of rotting vegetation was strong.

He was alerted to a nearness to man by the change in that smell. The first smell was that of campfire smoke that drifted slowly under the canopy of the forest. Next were the smells of cooking food. The noise of the camp could be heard.

He stopped his horse. Now that he was here, what was his best move? Reconnoiter was the first order of business.

He rode along the trail until he found an opening large enough to lead his horse off the beaten path. After a short walk from the trail he stopped and secured his horse. No one would see it unless searching for it. He took off his floppy-brimmed hat and hung it on the saddle horn. Thick forest was no place for this kind of headgear. He put his coonskin cap on.

"No noise, four-legged brother," Milton told his horse.

The horse flopped his ears as if he understood. Then he

dropped a hip, half drooped his eyelids, and drifted into a doze.

Milton moved quickly and quietly through the underbrush. Only alert animals of the forest heard him pass. He moved from location to location around the camp, searching out the one called Thumping Turtle. He could not be seen around the group of shacks that had been made of discarded items and brush. Most of the structures were nothing more than one-room hovels.

The breed could be gone from there, but Milton was not sure. He decided on a bold course of action. Many times a bold plan worked best.

He saw a mulatto woman standing beside a small campfire in front of a small shack. There was no one with her. He hoped there was no one inside the shack. If there were, he could take care of that problem.

The woman finished her coffee and went inside. The small structure was near the edge of the clearing. Milton would have a short distance to move from the forest to the shack.

Milton strode to the entrance and boldly walked in.

The woman sat on a makeshift chair. She gasped in surprise at his entrance, but she did not scream. She was alone. But she was too good looking to be without a man, and women were scarce in this land.

"Where's yore man?" he asked.

"I don't got one," she told him in chopped words.

"I don't wanna ask more than once," he informed her.

"He be gone. But you had better be careful. He be right back an' he don' lak nobody messin' wit' his woman," she told him as defiantly as she could.

"Where?"

"I don' know. He be gone all night," she informed him. His look caused her to continue. "He be on guard all night. He be back soon. Probably over drinkin' wit some of his so-called frien's."

Milton looked out the door. He could see no one coming in their direction.

"Yo gonna hurt me, mistuh?" she asked.

"Not if you don't give me cause," he assured her.

"I won't do such a thin'," she told him. A look of concern crossed her face. "What you want?"

"An Indian breed—Thumping Turtle by name," he said, looking around at the cluttered interior of the shack.

"Hey, yo' is a breed, too, ain' yo'?" She had just noticed. It was something most missed.

"I be one."

"I reckon I is too," she said. Then she asked again, "Yo' gonna hurt me?"

Milton was about to say something when he heard someone coming. He pulled out his tomahawk and looked at the woman. He shook his head slowly, indicating that it would be best to remain silent.

"Bessy, you got them clothes off, gal? It be a long night an' I needs some lovin'," the man called. He was white.

She stood up and called, "I be gittin' ready."

"I can see ya through the door. You got more clothes on than an ole maid at a church social." He laughed. "Git 'em off!"

She dropped her light shift and stood naked.

Milton approved of her action. This would disarm the man from acting quickly to danger.

The man ducked into the entrance and Milton struck him on the head with the flat of the blade. The woman caught him as he fell. Milton took a length of rawhide from around his waist and tied the man's hands behind his back.

The woman held the man's head against a golden breast. She pleaded, "Please, mistuh, don' kill us."

"I ain't here to kill you or him. I'm here for one man only," Milton informed her. "If I get him, I'll be on my way."

"I don' know who yo' be lookin' for." she said.

Thumping Turtle was not the kind you forgot or failed to

see. He was tall, a huge man, who would stand out in a crowd. And he was a woman's man. When he was sober, he always picked out the best-looking woman around. Milton figured this woman would fill the bill.

"I ain't gonna keep asking you. I don't mess with women-folks. But if I start on your man, he won't be needin' you or any other woman again," Milton told her in a hard tone.

"God! Yo' mean that, don' yo'?" she gasped.

"Every last word. He can live with that thing or without it." He didn't know why she was so surprised. The things this bunch did to people should make the most squeamish hard.

"Yo' say he name be Thumpin' Turtle?" she asked. She made no attempt to cover herself.

"That's right."

"He be here. He lef' two day ago," she informed him.

"You're sure?" he demanded.

"Sho' I be sho'. He spent de last night wid me. If'n it hadn't be fo' my man, thet big un wouldn't a had to pay." The woman smiled, remembering.

Yeah, he had been there all right. Satisfied women seemed to litter his trail. All except one woman.

The man moaned and tried to get up.

Milton took a rag and stuffed it in his mouth. Then he tied a cord of rawhide around his head to hold the gag in place. "You be still an' you're gonna live through this."

The man looked at him with uncomprehending, angry eyes.

"What yo' wan' dis mans fo'? This Thurmin' Turtle?" Bessy asked.

"He killed two men and a woman," he told her.

"God! He just up an kilt her?" She gasped.

That struck a chord.

"Yep. He's just that type," said Milton. "Especially if he gets a gutful of rum or whiskey."

"He got drunk as a lord here, but he didn' cause no trouble," she informed him. "Most Indians can't hold their likker."

"He left two days ago?" Milton asked, wanting to make sure how close he was getting.

"Yes, suh, it be two day now. He wuz too free wit' some of the wimmin here. So the mens tole him to git."

"Where?" demanded Milton.

For the first time she looked at her man. He shook his head violently for *No!*

"I want to know. If I don't find out right soon like, I'm gonna be the mad one," Milton told her. He didn't want to start yelling and scare her worse than she already was.

Both the man and woman looked at his tomahawk.

Milton used the edge of the tomahawk and shaved off part of the man's beard to show how sharp it was. It got the desired effect.

Fear crossed the man's eyes. But he still did not want the woman to talk.

The woman was ready and she was going to talk. "I tell! I tell you! He go south, down de main trail. He tole me he might be goin' back to Texas. I don' know fo' sho'."

"Thanks," Milton told her. He started to leave, but stopped. He looked at her with hard eyes. "Don't let him loose for a while."

"Naw, suh," she told him. Then she asked hopefully again, "Yo ain't gonna hurt us?"

He smiled, breaking the hardness of his eyes.

"Mistuh, I wanna tole you somethin' rat now," she said, grateful that he was really not going to do them injury. "Down dat trail, to de south, yo gonna come to a bigger camp. Maybe it be five or six mile from here. It be big camp. Bigger'n dis one. Yo git past dat camp, go past two trail further on and take the third to yo rite. Dat one takes yo to a place dat cross de river. Cross de river an' yo'll be in Texas. De trail to yo lef' go to Devil's Diggin's."

"Thanks," he told her, putting his tomahawk back into his belt.

"Thank yo' for not cuttin' my man," she said happily.

Her man looked less appreciative.

Milton slipped out of the camp and back to his horse.

His plan for getting through the camp was the same as for getting information, boldness. Old Andy Jackson always said, "Be bold! Take 'em by surprise!"

Milton figured most of the time Jackson was more bold than smart. He was going to be both.

Chapter Thirteen

Milton led his horse to the trail and remained on foot to lead him toward the camp. He stopped and tied his horse. He had to silence the guard, who was easy to find. He left the unlucky man unconscious and with an egg-sized knot on his head.

As he neared his horse, he heard the roar of a man coming from the direction of Bessy's shack. Either Bessy had turned the man loose or a friend had come by. No one could have broken loose from that rawhide on his own. If Bessy had been the one to turn him loose, Milton understood. She had to live with the animal.

Milton raced to his horse and climbed aboard. He rode into camp at a walk. He pulled the floppy hat down low over his eyes and rode calmly through the milling people. He rode as if he was in no hurry.

The loosened man ran across the camp, jumping up and down in his anger. He made more distance vertically than he did horizontally.

Bessy stood by the door of the shack, unconcerned about his anger. He would only do so much and that was all she would allow. No one manhandled her beyond what she would allow. Not more than once, as some men had learned the hard way.

Milton was halfway through the camp when the call came. "That's him! Texas law!" the angry man screamed.

Milton kicked his horse savagely. The surprised pony jumped forward and charged as he had been trained to do by his first master, a Comanche warrior. The pony was a horse bred and trained for war, and he reacted as such. The horse bowled over two men, making sure that at least one hoof hit each man. He bit a hunk of meat out of one man's shoulder and bit another man on the leg as he passed. The others quickly got the message and the group stampeded en masse from the path of the wild horse with gnashing teeth that had gone crazy. Some of the camp people did not stop running until they had gotten to their shacks.

Only a few in the camp had time to react in any manner. Only two shots were fired in Milton's direction, and both of those were wide of their marks. Others fired shots, but their targets were as diverse as the number of riflemen. There had to be more targets than one. No one would ride into camp alone.

The guard on the south side of the camp ran out into the middle of the trail. The charging horse, ears laid back, eyes wild, and lips baring snapping teeth, caused the guard to give way and jump back off the trail; but he hit some thick brush that flung him back on again. Milton swung his war ax and knocked the man unconscious with the flat of the blade. It wasn't a kind heart that kept him from killing the man, but he figured if he did so, his friends might feel obligated to avenge his death. He didn't need any extra problems at the moment.

He rode low in the saddle to make a smaller target and to dodge the low-hanging tree branches vaulting the trail. With a few strong jumps of his horse he was soon around a curve and hidden from the view of any rifleman in the camp.

Bessy's man stood in the middle of the camp, jumping up and down in place, screaming that he had been brutally treated. The men looked at him a moment, then they all went on about their business. Men were ordered to check the guards and give them assistance if it were needed.

"Reckon he be goin' to the main camp?" one of the men asked.

"Don't reckon even thet guy could be thet stupid," returned another. "Foolish an' downright stupid is somethin' else. They don' hire stupid lawmen."

"Reckon ya be right," the other man agreed.

Milton's visit would be forgotten, except by Bessy and her man.

After a short run he pulled his horse down to a single-footed pace the hardy pony could keep all day. He could also hear better at a slower gait.

Milton was not worried about the camp sending out a warning to the other camps. Any messenger would have to pass him on this narrow trail. And he doubted that the man he had tied up would tell them that he was on his way to the main camp. No one would believe him, and Milton had a feeling Bessy had more control over the situation than appeared on the surface.

He had ridden about four miles when he spotted two men at a cross in the trail. They set their horses on either side of the south-north trail and waited for him. The men had come onto the main trail from Milton's left, or from the east.

"How do?" greeted the older of the two men.

Milton nodded a greeting. He had not cocked the hammer of his long rifle, but his thumb was not far from its ear.

"I ain't seed ya aroun' here 'afore," the older man said.

Milton relaxed a little. He told them, "I ain't been around here before."

The younger of the two spit a stream of tobacco juice in front of Milton's horse.

"That a fact," replied the older man.

"Yep. Me an' them Mexican soldiers couldn't get an understandin' of one another. So I thought I'd mosey on," Milton told them.

"I know what you mean. I never did like thet damned place no how. Them Meskins let them damned Injuns and niggers run around jest like they wuz somebody," growled the older man. He lowered his rifle to let it rest on the neck of his horse.

"We Americans'll take over thet gawddamned place someday an' change hell outta thet," put in the younger man.

"Hey, I be Plunder. This is Plug. About all ya'll ever see

him do is chaw on a plug an' spit tobacco juice. So always stand upwind of him." Plunder laughed.

"I suppose you do all the plundering," Milton said with a smile.

"Haw, haw! You reckoned right, mister," Plunder continued to laugh.

"What ya be called?" Plug asked.

"Some call me Tall One," Milton told them.

"Ya look it all right, jest sittin' on thet hoss," Plunder agreed. "An', Mister Tall 'Un, that's a sad-looking hoss ya got there. Ain't meanin' no offense, now, don't ya know."

"Yeah, he do look kinda saddened some," agreed Milton. "I got him off a Comanche. The ole hoss didn't much want to part with his other owner, but I insisted. That's been five year ago an' he ain't ever got over it."

Plug spat another stream of tobacco juice, getting closer to the pony's front hooves. "Did the owner git over it?"

"He be too dead to consider it a problem," Milton informed him quietly.

"Wal, now, how the hell would ya feel if'n somebody up an' kilt yore master?" Plunder chuckled.

"I ain't ever gonna have no master," Plug informed him. "At no time, an' thet includes jail."

"Being as big as you air, I don't wonder the po' little hoss is plumb tuckered after five year of strugglin' under yore weight," grinned Plunder.

"What's thet sorry-lookin' critter's name?" asked Plug.

"Never named him. He's just a hoss," Milton told him.

"Hell, everthin' needs a name, even a ugly hoss," complained Plug.

"Tall 'Un, you must be okay to have got through the first camp. So let's be ridin' on," said Plunder.

"Lead out," offered Milton.

"Naw, you lead out. We want to keep an eye on thet poor ole nag of yours. Wouldn't want ya to be back behind us an'

thet poor ole thing keel over on ya. You'd be out a long walk,"
said Plunder. He shifted his rifle to his right hand.

Milton knew he was being put in front so they could watch
him. He heeled the pony and led out. He had no choice now
but to follow whatever lead was given and see where it took
him.

Chapter Fourteen

The second camp was a larger duplication of the first. The shacks were in no better condition and not better organized. They were so ill-kept and constructed so haphazardly that they were depressing. No red "savage" would be caught housing his dogs in such a structure, let alone his family.

Most of the camp's citizens were men, but there were a few women and children. Babes born out of the sanctity of civilization and into the world of outlawry.

The only building of any worth in the camp stood under a huge moss-covered oak tree near the center. It was constructed of logs with a shingled roof. It was an outlaw's "chapel," used as a meeting place, dance hall, and tavern. When the weather was good, dances were held outside in a smoothed-off dance ground.

The leader of the camp, which meant the one who controlled the physical power, lived in a lean-to connected to the end of the log building. He controlled not only the physical power, but also the wealth.

Two black men in ragged clothes sat at a workbench repairing boots and shoes. Blacks who ran to the Neutral Strip in hopes of freedom usually found themselves subverted to a different type of master. Blacks had also been stolen from their owners by armed force by outlaws of the Strip. The few free blacks had come in with other groups of outlaws and had their friends to back them up.

Plunder directed Milton to the front of the log building.

Three men came out of the lean-to. The man in the lead was

a short, wiry little man with a shock of red hair and a freckled face. He was the power in the camp.

Milton could understand why, if the little man controlled the two giants standing on either side of him. Both were well over six feet tall, broad of chest, with arms like small tree trunks and ham-size hands. As if on order, the two stopped, a respectful step in back of the little man, and folded their arms across their chests.

"What ye two cotched here, Plunder?" the red top asked in a Scottish accent.

"How do, Big Red? Oh, we found him back on the trail, ridin' this mean little Injun pony," Plunder informed him.

"How do, Big Red," greeted Plug, following that with a well-aimed stream of tobacco juice that hit the tail of Milton's horse.

I owe you one, mister, thought Milton.

"That is a poor-lookin' critter he be ridin', ain't it?" asked Plug.

"Th' horse may be thet, mon, but th' critter thet be riddin' him is quite impressive," said Big Red.

Big Red. Milton laughed inside. But he figured if a man controlled those two giants standing on either side, then he could demand to be called anything he wished.

"What they call ye, tall mon?" demanded Big Red.

"Tall One," Milton said simply.

"Th' tall, dark, silent type, eh?" growled Big Red. "Whar ye be from, Tall One?"

"From all over," Milton informed him.

Big Red bristled.

"He jest come outta Texas," offered Plunder.

"Is thet a fact?" asked Big Red, his voice full of sarcasm. Then he asked Milton, "Do ye know Haden Edwards, mon?"

"I do." Milton sat his horse easily. If he had to fight his way out of this, he was not sure if he would make it alive. But he would damned sure give a good account of himself.

"Who do he ride wit', mon?" The glower on Big Red's face made his freckles larger with more of a red tint.

"Nobody. He clerks in the mercantile he owns with his son-in-law, Frost Thorn, in Nacogdoches," replied Milton.

"Ye know lot aboot 'em, don't ye?" growled Big Red.

"Everybody in East Texas knows that," Milton told him, no give in his voice. If he was going down, it would be just like always, standing and giving back what he got.

"You know Vicente Cordova, too, mon?" Big Red asked dryly.

"Only in passin'. He was primary judge an' has been the cap'n of the local militia at Nacogdoches fer a good while. I keep clear of cap'ns an' armies," Milton told him. "Do you know Don Vicente?"

Big Red ignored the question. "He might not be from th' States. We want to make sure there are no spies in our camp."

"Well, hell, Big Red, ast him if'n he is," suggested Plunder.

"Plunder, ye is one of the more dumbest bastids in this har camp," Big Red snarled, his green eyes flashing. "An' I do the tellin' what to do an' what not to do aroun' here."

"Okay, Big Red. I wuz jest tryin' to help," mumbled Plunder.

"If I need help, I'll git help from some critter that kin do th' job. I damned sure won't choose such as ye," spat the red-headed camp leader.

Love and respect among thieves. Milton grinned inwardly.

Plug spat another stream of tobacco juice, but he kept his peace. He didn't have enough brotherly love for Plunder to face Big Red. In fact, he didn't have any love, brotherly or otherwise, for his sidekick.

"Why did ye leave Texas?" asked Big Red, still angry about something.

Milton figured he woke every morning mad about something. Maybe he felt he was shorter than nature should have made him.

"I got tired of Piedras's soldier boys," replied Milton.

The huge man to Big Red's left said something in a low voice. Big Red nodded. "Lion Jaw says he's seen you someplace, mon. He ain't sure where, but he thinks it was in Texas."

Milton sat his horse, noncommittal. He hoped the small giant was wrong.

"Why should I believe ye be from Texas?" asked Big Red, still not sure about Milton.

Milton shrugged his shoulders. *That's your problem, little man.*

"Big Red, we found him on the trail comin' from Jake's camp. He couldn't a got past there if'n somethin' wuz wrong with him," Plug put in.

"An' jest who ever said Jake was the smartest person in the world?" spat the redhead. Big Red looked at Plug a moment, at Milton, and then at Plunder. "Okay, Plunder, ye an' Plug found this stray won, so ye take him to your shack an' take care of him," ordered Big Red. "An' tall mon, we got rules in this camp. We ain't a bunch of savage heathens. No stealin', no messin' wit other mon's wimmin without jest compensation, an' no nothin' thet ain't allowed. Those two boneheads will give the rule to ye. An', tall mon, I suppose ye done got the drift as to who be boss in this camp?"

Milton sat his horse, noncommittal.

"We got him, Big Red," Plunder assured him. "Come on, Tall 'Un."

As they rode off, Big Red yelled, "Ye two brung him, so ye two air responsible for him!"

"Got it," returned Plunder, then mumbled something under his breath.

"Some of these days, Plunder, thet sawed-off bastard ain't gonna 'ave them two giants handy," said Plug when they got out of hearing.

"Yeah, but he got others, Plug. They're as mean as those two 'cause there's more of 'em," Plunder reminded him.

"Our time is a comin' someday," Plug assured his sidekick.

Plunder led through the camp and among the maze of

shacks. People stopped to watch them pass. A stranger was among them and people in their profession were nervous and suspicious of strangers.

Milton would find himself in a real fix if someone remembered that he had ridden with Austin's boys against outlaws and Waco Indians. But they might just think of him as another one of those men who spent their lives on the side of the law that was most convenient at the moment.

They did not know it, but he was one of those men who did as he wished. Sometimes he followed the setting sun. Sometimes he rode facing the rising sun. But no matter what he did, he would always follow the gun and adventure. He tried to stay within the law, but he had his own code to follow. That code came from a mixture of his Cherokee and Anglo-Saxon heritages. Texas gave him a place to practice that code.

Plunder stopped before a brush-covered lean-to. It was not even a shack. The front of the lean-to was practically open to the elements. The two ends were walled in by discarded lumber and tree limbs. The roof was seven feet high at the front and sloped to the ground in the rear. Old sailcloth was used to aid in waterproofing the roof. A sheet or two of tarp made up the roof's ceiling. The lean-to was built for sleeping and getting out of the rain. The rest of the time was spent outdoors.

"This here's home sweet home," Plunder informed Milton.

"Best one I ever had," said Plug.

"Hell, it's the onliest one ya ever had," Plunder reminded him.

"Thet's right," Plug agreed. He said to Milton, "Make yoreself to home, tall man. Ya kin share anythin' we got, 'cept air woman."

"An' if ya got 'nough money, ya can share her," laughed Plunder. "Money kin buy or rent most anythin' we got."

" 'Cept hosses," Plug corrected.

"Hell, I said jest 'bout everythin'. Gawddamn! Everybody knows hosses is sacred to a feller," Plunder reminded him.

"An' speakin' of our woman, I wonder where thet Injun bitch is?"

"She'd better not try to escape again. I ain't gonna be none too happy trompin' through them swamps," growled Plunder. "I'm sorry we ever got hooked up with thet bitch. But no, ya jest had to kill them two guys to git her. She's been a gawddamn pain in the ass ever since."

"She may be trouble at times, but she's makin' us more money than we kin steal. She makes more money than we ever had before," Plug informed him. "An' I seed you can't stay off top of her."

"Thet's what them Injun wimmin are made for," said Plunder, pulling his belt up over his potbelly. His week-old beard was shot with gray hair. His dark-brown teeth were stained beyond repair. There was a twinkle in his eyes as he thought about women in bed.

"An' she does the cookin'," Plug put in.

"It ain't worth one bit of it sometimes," commented Plunder, forgetting the pleasure of her company when he thought of the trouble. "Wonder where she is, nohow?"

"Who knows what in the gawddamned hell them Injun wimmin ever do?" growled Plug. He was getting mad. "She'd better be out makin' us some money. I give her orders to 'ave some waitin'."

"Damned Injun woman would bed down with anybody," Plunder said.

"Ain't thet a gawdamned fact. She beds down with the both of us," Plug said dryly.

Milton had found out years before why the Mexicans called the American Anglos "Anglos *goddames!*" Take the word away from most Anglos and they'd be dead within a week.

The tall Texan led his horse off to one side and tied him to a limb hanging down from a huge pecan tree. He looked up and saw that it was going to produce a large harvest of nuts this season. A squirrel sniffed its nose at the smell of the newcomers and then scampered out of sight.

"Hey, Tall 'Un, don' get off too far," warned Plunder.

Milton didn't bother to comment. He pulled the saddle off his horse and dropped it and the rest of his gear in the spot where he would set up his own camp. He was not going to get any closer to Plug and Plunder than was necessary.

The horse looked around at him with a look that seemed to say, *It's about time you quit for the day. How long is this break gonna last?*

Milton ignored him.

A woman walked up to the lean-to without greeting the men. She walked directly to the fire and blew the coals into a flame. The woman was on the heavy side and near her middle years.

"Wal, hello there, Morning Light, you be a good girl?" Plunder greeted her, slapping her on her generous rump.

Morning Light ignored him.

"Ain't glad to see us, be she?" grinned Plug. He walked over to her and held out his hand.

She handed him the money she was holding.

"Wal, now. See here? She got more money then I tole her to git," Plug said in appreciation. "Who says a Injun woman don't like to bed down with us white men?"

She probably wanted to keep from getting a beating, thought Milton.

Morning Light continued to busy herself around the fire. She wore a red skirt that was bordered in a blue design. The skirt had lost its bright color long ago. Her white blouse was no longer white, but clean, even though it was stained from the lack of bleach and soap. There was no smell about her person, indicating that she bathed regularly.

"Where-all you be, woman?" asked Plunder, not expecting an answer.

"Thet gawddamned Injun ain't ever gonna learn no English. She's like all of 'em. She ain't smart enough to learn a civilized tongue," growled Plug, spitting a stream of tobacco juice in the direction of the fire.

Milton looked at him a moment. Now he knew which one was the woman beater. Plug's little blue Anglo-Saxon eyes spoke more than words and his attitude verified the fact. The man's often sullen attitude and stern looks at people spoke of the mean streak in his nature. A mean streak he vented on those weaker than himself.

Plunder was a larger version of Plug, except his disposition was not as sullen and he let Plug do the manhandling. He tended to make a display of laughing at himself and the rest of the world. He would laugh while he cut a breast off an Indian woman with the intention of making a new tobacco pouch out of it. Both men were illiterate.

Milton felt the same about them as he did a stray dog that occasionally bit someone on the streets. He would just as soon see them taken off the streets for good.

Morning Light glanced at Milton. That one glance told her that he was a breed. He looked all right to her, but breeds were worse than pure bloods, white or red, at times. They seemed to have a mad on all the time and felt everyone was the cause of their problems with the two races.

Plunder walked over to Morning Light, who was bending over the fire, and flipped her skirt up over her back. "Hey, tall man, see what you gonna miss if'n you don't got money?"

Morning Light pulled her skirt back down and kept on cooking the food.

Milton stowed his saddle and bedroll and he walked over to the fire. He asked in the Choctaw trade language, "Who are your people?"

"Quapaw," she told him with a Siouan accent. She used the term her people used for their tribe. Others called them Arkansas, "People down the river."

"Are your people now in Texas?" he asked. He knew that a group of the Quapaw had come to Texas.

"I do not know. We were going to join the rest of our people on the Red River. These Neutral Strip dogs caught me."

"Hey, what kind of heathern talk is thet? Speak American

round me. You be an Indian man or something? Maybe a squaw man?" asked Plug.

"We're using Choctaw trade language. Everybody in the southern part of the States uses it," Milton informed him.

"Wal, we be from upstate New York," Plunder informed him. "All we speak is American."

"I suggest you learn a trade language or Spanish if you aim to stay around here," Milton suggested.

Plug spat another stream of tobacco juice and growled, "Let 'em learn American or we ain't gonna talk to 'em."

Milton shrugged. It made no difference to him how they made out in the world. It was amazing they had lasted this long.

"An' only English is to be used round here," Plug ordered.

Milton turned slowly to face him and fixed the unkempt man with a cold, ice-blue stare. "Mister, no one tells me who to talk to, when to talk, or in what language. Never."

The tone of Milton's voice spoke volumes about where he stood on the subject.

It was Plug's turn to shrug his shoulders. "Talk to who an' in what tongue ya want."

Milton looked at Morning Light. "Do you understand English?"

"Yes."

Milton nearly burst out laughing. He went to his bedroll and returned to the fire with salt, coffee, and meat for her to use.

She smiled her appreciation. Then she asked in a low voice, "You not outlaw man like these dogs?"

"No."

"Good. What your people?"

"Tsalagi."

"Oh, Cherokee man. When you leave, Tall Man, I go with you," she informed him.

He nodded his head that he understood, but he was thinking, *Oh, hell!* But she deserved to get out of this place, and out of the clutches of these two. And if she really wanted to go, he would do anything and everything possible to see that she was free to leave this place.

As he left the lean-to, Plunder called to him, "Hey, Tall 'Un, ya ain't got free run of the camp yet?"

"You think I'm gonna go somewhere afoot?" Milton asked.

"Wal, I don't reckon you'd git very far. Jest as long as ya stay outta Big Red's way. We don' need his kind a trouble," Plunder told him.

The two outlaws would worry about Milton being afoot if they knew the Tall Man could run fifty miles a day, day after day.

Plug looked after Milton. "I still think he's an Injun."

"Naw, he's too damned smart to be a Injun. You see how good a English he talks? Ya know there ain't no heathern redskins smart 'nough to talk American thet good. Not even a breed," Plunder assured Plug.

"When he comes back, I'm gonna see if'n he can read this here paper. That oughta do it," said Plug with a humorless grin.

"Wal, gawddamn, Plug, jest how in hell ya gonna knowed if'n he kin read or not? You don' know what thet damned thin' says any more than I do." Plunder laughed.

"Plunder, we might be frien's ever since I wuz knee high to Grandma's duck, but I'm gonna knock hell outta ya some of these days for bein' so damned know-it-all talkative," Plug complained to his partner.

"Lak hell you will. An' okay, mister smart-ass, so how ya gonna know if'n he can read or he can't?" asked Plunder with a smirk.

"If'n he kin read it, then he'll do it. If'n he can't, well, hell, we'll know thet too," said Plug, stomping off for the log house. He needed somebody smarter to talk to. "Ya coming?"

Plunder already had his hand up Morning Light's dress,

rubbing hard, trying to excite her. She went about her work, ignoring him the best she could.

"Naw, me an' Morning Light's got some business to tend to. An' it ain't readin' an' talkin' business," laughed Plunder.

"Gawddamn!" Plug grumbled under his breath.

Chapter Fifteen

Milton walked around the camp, getting the lay of the land. He checked out the location of the guards at both entrances to the camp. They were no more alert than the guards had been at the first camp.

He carried his long rifle cradled in the crook of his left arm. The outlaws went about camp without their rifles, but most of them carried at least one weapon in their belts. The favorites were knives, Indian trade-tomahawks, and pistols. A couple of men carried short swords. Milton felt he should keep his rifle at hand until it could be determined if the other camp had sent someone here to warn them that Texas law was on the loose. He smiled at that. Him the law.

Most of the men in the camp were from the United States and a few of European origin. Women were few, but those came from many different stations in life. A few were there of their own volition; most were like Morning Light, they had been abducted to cook for the men and take care of their sexual needs. The children of these unions became people who knew no other world. After a few years in the camp, the women were too ashamed and used-up to try going back home.

Two Indians sat against the trunk of a tree, looking on the confusion and filth of the camp with noncommittal dark eyes. Each had his own reason for being there, the reasons as varied as the men. Each grunted as Milton passed. Both were members of the once powerful Caddo Confederation.

The underbrush had been cleared over the years from under

the heavy canopied trees. It had been cleared to build lean-tos and for firewood, not out of orderliness.

What a dirty, disorganized camp, thought Milton. Even the Osages were cleaner than this.

There was a little discrimination in everyone.

Milton walked past a lean-to where a group of men sat passing the jug and telling tall tales.

"Hey, who be ya an' where ya bound?" one called to Milton.

Milton continued to walk past.

"Hey, you ain't thet big, mister. They's be a lot of us round here. Don't go thinkin' ya own any part of this place," a huge man yelled.

Milton stopped and turned toward the men. There was a hint of a smile on his dark face. These men went through life from one confrontation to another. Most of them were here, in the Strip, because they just couldn't get along with the rest of society. Peace-loving men and lazy men tend to go with the flow. A coward did the best he could in all situations. The brave and the hardy confronted the sassy and the brassy, adding spice and interest to life.

"It's best to be friendly, tall man," another said with a laugh.

"Mon, ye air a big one, ye air," said a man in a tam-o'-shanter. He seemed to be of a better disposition than his countryman, Big Red.

"He is a tall 'un, ain't he," agreed another one.

"He is a big one to us wee Scotsmen," the tam-o'-shanter assured him.

Milton stood, not making any response one way or the other.

"You as tough as you act, mister?" a man asked.

"He looks lak he be pretty tough to me, Jackknife," another laughed.

"Wit' six of us'uns here? He ain't so tough," Jackknife growled, tough like.

The new dog in town. All of them would have to take a sniff.

"My legs is as big as yore body, boy," a huge man laughed. He sat on a log, a tin cup balanced in his hand. "I is the big boy aroun' here. So I be the one thet pisses on the campfars."

Trouble, Milton thought. Handle it now or forget it.

"I jest might take thet long rifle away from ya an' spank yore dirty little ass," the huge man told Milton.

Milton stepped forward and butt-stroked the huge man with the butt of his rifle as the man was raising the cup to his mouth. The rifle stock hit the cup, driving it viciously into his face. Blood gushed from the cut made by the edge of the tin cup, cutting a half moon through the bridge of his nose.

With a roar the man stood up to do battle. Milton slipped the tomahawk from his belt and hit the man on the head with the flat part of the blade. It took a second blow to fell him.

"Damn! I knowed ole big 'un had a hard head. But, man, didn' think it would to take two blows like thet," one of the men said in amazement.

"Wal, I'll be gawddamn! Ole Bear Growl's is out hisself like a pissed-on campfar," the first man stated.

"An' smells just as bad, mon," tam-o'-shanter commented.

"He be out an' thet's fer a fact. I ain't never seed nobody put away thet fast. An' I ain't never seed ole Bear Growl be put away at-all," said the first man. "Sit, mister, it'd be a pleasure to buy ya a drink."

He was accepted.

These men respected brute force above all things. That was the reason Big Red was the boss of the camp. He controlled the camp's brute force.

No one offered to give aid to Bear Growl. If he bled to death or drowned in his own blood, that was his own fault.

Milton accepted the drink handed him in a none-too-clean glass jar.

"I be Jesse," the first man introduced himself. "This feller wit' the funny hat is Scotty. These others air Jackknife, Rover, an' Crip. Course, ya already met up wit ole Bear Growl."

Scotty was dressed with clothing from his home in Scotland mixed with American frontier garb. Crip had gotten his name from his deformed left leg. Milton learned Rover had earned his name from many travels. Jackknife spent his time carving with his jackknife, on both wood and people. Jesse was the only one to use his given name.

"Where you be from, stranger?" Jackknife asked.

"They call me Tall One. Texas."

"Over Mexico way, eh, mon?" Scotty asked, making it more of a comment.

"We gonna go over there someday an' run thet place. Take it plum away from them Meskins," Jackknife assured him.

"Is it true them Meskins let niggers and Injuns own land?" asked Crip.

"Yep, they do," Milton informed him.

"Gawd!" was his shocked comment. Crip was not as bright as most people. But not many in the camp was overly bright by normal standards.

"Hell, who ever said them Meskins is real people?" asked Rover.

Laughter.

"Ain't thet a fact," said Jackknife, knowing he was a cut above the best "Meskin" going.

"Yeah, them Spanish kilt off all of 'em Indians, jest about, an' stole all their land an' gold. Them's what's left, they's be treated like true citizens," Jesse told them.

"They've got to. Them redskins has been converted to the Church of Rome. They can't turn 'em out. The pope'd kick all of 'em outta his church," the well-traveled Rover informed them.

"Is it true thet them priests spend the first night wit the gal when she git married?" asked Crip, holding out his tin cup for a refill.

Milton laughed inside. It wasn't a laugh of joy or humor.

The ignorance of some people bordered on plain out-and-out stupidity. "I don't know. I ain't never been married."

"Lucky suno'abitch," returned the grinning Jesse.

"I was married once, me boys," Scotty informed them. "I found me favorite ewe was a better roll in the hay than that bag o' bones they called me wife."

"You ever been down San Antonio way?" Crip asked Milton.

"Yep."

"Boy, you shore Injun up round folks, don't ya?" complained Jackknife.

"Maybe he be Indian," replied Scotty.

"The way he handles hisself, he kin be a gawddamned yaller Chinee boy if'n he want," Jessie assured them.

"Ain't thet a fact," agreed Crip.

Rover got up from the stump he was sitting on and went to refill his cup. He scratched his crotch as he walked. It seemed that all the men were infected by lice, crabs, and something called a venereal disease. They did not know the source, or what to do about it even if they knew how to find out.

"Me an' this feller named Skinner went to San Antonio one time. Fact is, thet be my onliest time. 'Bout three year ago it were. Hit weren't much of a town. Big name, little place. But it do have two things we took to rite off. Wimmin an' booze. Man alive! Them peppers shore keeps them Meskin gals het up!" Rover advised them.

"I do like het-up gals," admitted Jesse.

"Hell! I like any kind of gals," Crip told them.

Laughter.

"They had this drink they made outta cactus," the storyteller tried to continue.

"They pull the thorns off?" asked Jackknife, beginning to feel the effects of the rotgut camp whiskey.

"It felt like they did till mornin' come. Then ya knowed they didn', or them buggers sprouted in the night. Anyhow, it tooken a small barrelful to git ole' Skinner drunk. An', Gawd, what a drunk! It was one of them kinda dumb, stupor drunks. All of ya guys thet knowed ole Skinner knowed he had a head start on dumb an' stupor 'afore he drank a thing." Rover laughed.

The men joined him with their laughter as if they knew Skinner personally.

"Wal, thet cactus juice locked on his mind lak a grip of a grizzly bar. He couldn't move, jest sit there. Not even his eyes moved. He jest sat." Rover took another drink of the camp's corn squeezings before he continued.

"I wuz well on the way to gettin' drunk myself. I seed thet an' cut it off. It did some good, but it didn't last long," Rover admitted. "It be hard to sit there with all thet booze an' not drink it."

"You have one of them Meskin señoritas?" asked Crip, interested in places he had never been. Especially about its women.

"Hell, I ain't had nothin' thet night. Next thing I knowed, it was daylight next day. Some kid wuz sweepin' up the cantina. I could open my eyes, but I still couldn't move worth a damn. Jest lak I wuz plum locked in place." Rover paused and suddenly ran his hand down inside his pants and scratched viciously.

"Ole Skinner come outta it. He didn' wanta pee or anythin'. He jest wanted another drink," Rover continued after the scratching session. "Wal, he looked round thet joint till he found a big jar. He picks it up an' pigs it down like he does everthin'. All a sudden like, he turns green, then purple. He starts spittin' an' sputterin'. Drops thet big jar. *Bam!* It broke all to hell. Skinner then turns the damnedest red I ever seed. I could see he weren't able to breath. You know, I sat there an' watched ole Skinner croak."

"Ya mean he upped and died?" asked Crip in disbelief.

"Deader'n hell before Judgment Day," Rover assured him.

"My Gawd! Did they poison him, do you reckon?" asked Jackknife.

"Naw, weren't as excitin' as all thet. Thet cantina keeper

tole me thet jar held some of the peppers called jalapeño, not booze. They et 'em all the time down there. Thet's why they called 'pepper-bellies.' All thet juice did ole' Skinner in. I lef' him down on the creek, buried deep. Wal, a couple of feet," Rover finished.

"Good Gawd Almighty damn! Done in by a pepper!" Jackknife exclaimed in amazement. It was hard to believe. "Thet's kinda hard to take."

"Hell, when yore done in, yore done in, no matter what done it," Jesse told him.

"Yes, mon, but by peppers?" asked Scotty.

"Them ain't the normal, run-of-the-mill peppers, boys. This 'uns the catty wompus of all them peppers," Rover assured them.

"Do you know about them peppers, Tall One?" asked Crip.

"Yep. They're plenty hot, all right. But even the little Mexican kids eat 'em."

"I'll be damned in January," said Crip.

"Hell, Crip, you'd be damned anytime," put in Jackknife.

The men laughed at Crip's expense.

Milton passed the glass jar to the storyteller. He deserved it. Milton stood up. "Thank ye for the drink an' story, gentlemen."

He had done his duty.

"Yore more than welcome, stranger," replied Jackknife.

"Anybody who'd put ole Bear Growl low is welcome to more," said Jesse.

"Yeah, we got plenty," put in Crip.

"Thanks, but I think I'll hunt me up a feed," Milton told them.

"Hey, Tall 'Un, come to the dance tonight fer the blowout. We're gonna tie a ribbon round the heifer's tail an' watch her jump over the moon," invited Rover.

"An' we're gonna howl at it," laughed the already drunk Jackknife.

Milton waved a hand in parting.

The man he had hit with his tomahawk still lay unconscious. No one cared about his hurts. The longer he was out,
the less he would drink.

Chapter Sixteen

Morning Light had supper prepared when Milton returned. She had done the best she could with what she had. Her two men keepers were not the best providers she had seen. Those two were not the best of anything she had ever seen. But they were always around at mealtime, continually complaining about lack of meat or something.

"Set an' eat," Plunder invited, chewing on the piece of meat Milton had provided.

Plunder and Plug ate the way they did all things, sloppily.

When they had finished eating, the men lit their pipes and topped off their food with a drink of rum.

Milton's pipe was an old clay he had had for years. It had gone through his kind of life in one piece so far.

"Hey, Tall 'Un, we air fixin' to go to the dance. So lets get on with it," Plunder told him.

"I want to let the meal settle first. I'll be there later," said Milton.

"We should go together," Plunder argued.

"Aw, hell, Plunder, let him be. He kin come when Mornin' Light comes," said Plug. Then he gave a vulgar laugh, "That is, if'n she don't git ya in 'tween them blankets an' makes ya forget."

"I'd shore be hot 'tween them blankets." Plunder laughed.

"An' don't forget the money," Plug directed to Morning Light. She looked dumb and he stomped off. "Aw, shit!"

Plunder laughed at it all and followed Plug.

"Don' let her git too close to a knife if she gets mad, Tall

'Un. She'll change the pitch of yore voice," Plunder called with a laugh.

The men walked along, making vulgar gestures and telling dirty stories.

"Why are you here, Tall One?" Morning Light asked as soon as the two departed.

"I'm looking for someone," he told her.

"Is he in this camp?" she asked, going about cleaning up around the cook fire.

"I haven't seen him here. If he was here, I would have known by now," he told her.

"Do you search for this man for white man's law or the clan law of the Cherokee?" she asked, looking at him.

"Both my law and the white man's law. If he does not fight me, I will take him to white man's law. If he fights . . ." Milton shrugged his shoulder.

"This man is a bad one, huh?" asked Morning Light, wondering what would make this man chase after someone in such dangerous places.

"He killed a woman," he told her simply.

"Ah, Cherokee manhood has been affronted, eh? You Cherokee men do think highly of your women. Neither you nor no other man can lay an angry hand on your little pets," she said in a mocking voice.

"She was a Mexican settler's wife," he informed her, cleaning the burnt tobacco out of his pipe. When he'd finished, he put it in its wooden case and placed it in his saddlebags.

Her eyes followed him until he returned to sit cross-legged in front of her. "What? A white woman? You risk being killed for a white woman?"

"She was a woman nonetheless. A Texas woman. A woman from the place I now call my own," he informed her. "When a man beats or kills a woman, I react."

She studied him a moment. Yes, he spoke the truth. He was a typical Cherokee warrior who would champion any cause or go a thousand miles on foot in the dead of winter just for a new war name. Her people had spoken many times about the relentless war these people made on those they did not like or wished to bring clan justice upon. They were a fearsome people when on the warpath. The Quapaw scared their children or threatened them with the bad Cherokee chief called Tahchee, or "Dutch" by the whites.

It seemed that Indian breeds were not much different from the warriors they were reared by. Even though this one did seem educated in the white man's way and very civilized, he had a look about him that spoke of another side. After all, civilization was only skin deep in all people. Put a man in a place where he can act uncivilized, and that is how he will act. She had to go no farther than this bunch around her.

She asked, "Is it true that a Cherokee man will stand and let any Cherokee woman beat on him?"

Milton tried his hand at some dry humor. "Not this breed. I'll run."

"Your white blood doesn't get in the way of how you think?"

"On that part, not so far," said Milton. "If it does, it'll be time for someone to send me to the Black Man in the West."

She shook her head. Then she asked, "You going to take me to the blankets?"

"I won't follow those two. And I haven't been asked," he replied.

She smiled. "I don't blame you. I wouldn't follow those two either. Okay, breed man, who do you seek?"

"A Coushatta breed called Thumping Turtle," he informed her.

"Ah!"

"You have seen him?" That man got around. And between every blanket in sight.

"Yes," she told him with a smile.

"You say 'ah' as if it were with pleasure," he remarked.

"Only slightly. One of the girls here told me of him. Ah, to have one such as he for your own," sighed Morning Light.

Then she sobered and her forehead wrinkled. "He killed a woman?"

"He did."

"Drunk?" she asked, knowing the cause of most family problems among Indians.

"As ten Indians," he assured her.

"The slop of the white man! The vile slop!" she spat, anger and disgust in her voice. "White man's evil water will be the ruin of the Indian. It will tear down the tribal system. Then it will tear down the family system. Then we are finished. White men do not need to shoot us. Send more whiskey and missionaries among us. We are dead."

There was great anguish in her voice. He felt saddened.

But he had a job that needed getting done. He asked. "Thumping Turtle, where is he?"

"He was here. He goes now, back across the river to Texas," she said, wiping her hands on a rag.

"Okay. Then I must follow," he informed her.

"Remember, tall man, when you go, I go. I be with my people again and my family," she told him in a voice that would stand for no disagreement.

"I wouldn't go without you. I'll see that you get to your people," he promised. No one deserved being held by this bunch.

"I believe it. If you tell me, I believe it," she said in a pleased voice.

"How long have you been away from your people?" he asked.

"Over three years. Maybe four now. Who counts?" she asked him.

"You tried to escape a few times, so I hear."

"Yes, but I get caught every time. This forest is too thick. It is easy to get lost. We are surrounded by water. The few trails are well guarded. It is impossible to get out," she told him. "It makes Plug mad every time I try. The fifth time I tried, he threw me down and cut the nipple from my left breast. I stopped running for a while. But I tried five more times. Plunder told him he could not cut me any more, more cuts would disfigure my body too much and they could not sell me anymore. Money means more to Plug than revenge or honor."

That little bastard needs my attention, thought Milton. *Someday, little man, someday you will get my full attention.*

"I know I will escape someday. I know it. That is what keeps me going and I don't lay down someplace and give up," she told him, hope in her voice. "One day a man came to the camp. He told me he was once a spirit man of the whites. He got into trouble out there someway, I don't know. This man liked me. He came to my blankets many times. Then he tells me that he will try to get me away. Who knows? Maybe he still had some of his spirit-man powers.

"We don't even get to the edge of camp. Plug caught us. This once-upon-a-time spirit man, he tells Plug that I made him come. Plug sent me back here. He beat me good. I don't ever see this spirit man again, but I heard screams all night. I was told it was him."

He growled, "Dogs."

"No, not dogs. Only humans act like him," Morning Light told him sadly.

"Be ready anytime," he informed her.

"Maybe tonight, huh?"

"Could be," he said, not promising anything.

"I be ready, breed man. You just do your job."

He smiled.

Milton left her by the fire. He left his long rifle and horse pistol behind. Both the guns and his horse would be safe in his camp. Not only would that four-legged critter make sure he remained where he was tied, there was no stealing here in camp. That was one of the first rules. It had always been an unwritten law among outlaws. Steal anything and everything from outsiders that was not tied down, but never steal from another outlaw you lived with.

The only weapons he carried were his trusty tomahawk and

Bowie knife stuck in his belt. He seldom ventured far completely naked.

Pine-knot torches lit the cleared area in front of the log building. Split log planks served as an outside bar, although most of the men had brought their own jugs. But the bar was doing a brisk business selling homemade beer, which was controlled by Big Red and company.

Men and women danced on the smooth ground. Because of the shortage of women, some of the men danced together.

The music consisted of three fiddles, a banjo, an accordion, two guitars, and a squeaking bagpipe. It was not concert music, but it made little difference to the dancers. The musicians themselves seemed each to be playing in a world all his own, regimenting himself with the others only for the sake of the same song.

A woman, deep in her cups, pulled her skirt high over her head and danced around and around. She was having a great time and simultaneously showing off her wares to prospective customers. She and her man would make a lot of money off this shindig. Some of the women could handle twenty men or more before the night was over.

The same two Caddo Indians Milton had seen on his walk around camp were sitting with their backs against a huge moss-covered oak tree. Both men sat with a bottle between their legs. These were not the cup-drinking kind.

Both men were long past being Caddo warriors. They were dirty and their clothing was in bad need of repair. The two Indians spent most of their time drinking up what they earned by hunting.

What was it Morning Light had just said? "White men do not need to shoot us. Send more whiskey and missionaries."

One grunted a greeting as Milton walked past. He stopped and said in Spanish, "How is it with you, cousins?"

He could not force himself to call them brothers.

"We are happy."

"We have the liquid of happiness. Do you wish to partake, brother?"

"No. Tonight I do not drink," Milton told them.

"Huh, has the priest got to you? Has he told you how vile this liquid of happiness is?"

The man did not want an answer nor did he really care.

"How are you two here in this white man's camp?" asked Milton.

"We are the camp's hunters. We bring meat. White men don't like to hunt. We do. We keep them happy," the older man told him.

I bet you two are great hunters, thought Milton.

"And these white men pay for what my woman would give for nothing. We have truly fallen upon good times, we two," said the younger man.

Milton looked at the two in the failing light. They represented what kept him from looking too deeply into the bottom of the cup.

"What are you doing here, brother?" asked the younger man.

"Passing through."

"You speak Spanish well," he commented.

"I live in Texas," Milton informed them.

"Ah, many of our people are in what the white man calls Texas," remarked the older man.

"When did you learn Spanish so well?" Milton asked them.

"When the Spanish were here, their spirit men taught us," the older man said. He took a drink from his jug bottle and shuddered.

Liquid dreams. Milton shook his head.

"They say there is an invisible line between here and Texas, dividing the Caddo people. I know of no invisible line," growled the younger man. "I have not been told of an invisible line that divides our people's land. If anyone would know about this line, it would be we Caddo. We have been here since the beginning of time."

"Yes, but the white man keeps moving things around," complained the older man. "No one knows where anything belongs anymore."

"The old men didn't tell me of any invisible line," the younger man said, still stuck on the invisible line.

The older man looked up toward Milton. "The white man sends his diseases ahead to kill for him. They have that power. The old men told me of this. The white man can let loose his disease spirit even among his own people to kill those he doesn't like. That is a bad way to kill a fellow human."

The older man took a long drink from his bottle and shook violently again. He sat a moment, thinking of another time and another place. "The white spirit-men let loose their disease and now all my living family generations are gone. My grandfathers, my grandmothers, my father, my mother, wife, brothers, sisters, children, cousins, all. I am the last of my family, for all of my children are gone. After me there will be no more."

"He speaks a fact," the younger man said. "All of my babies died, except one. Then the Kickapoo came and killed it. The white spirit man that came among us said that our Father, the Creator, was punishing me for being a heathen. Now my woman cannot give me a son. Is he right, do you think?"

Questions asked, no answers given.

"Why are you here?" the younger man asked again.

"Just passing through," Milton repeated.

"Do you want a drink?" the older man asked.

"No. Not tonight," Milton told him, and walked away.

The camp hunters! The camp's pimps and drunks, thought Milton. But there was a sadness in his heart for these men. It lay hot and hard on his heart. There was no way to cool it or make it soft. Old ways and old people were passing before the onslaught of time and another society. It was a sad thought. It was even sadder when you were living it.

"Hey, tall man, come on over for a drink of this liquid fire," a man called. It was Jesse.

"Be obliged to visit, but I ain't drinking tonight, gentlemen," Milton told them.

"Still the new one in the pack an' ain't pissed on the trees to mark off a spot, huh?" asked Rover with a laugh.

"He's got a good start. He shore pissed on Bear Growl," Jesse told them in admiration.

There was much laughter and slapping of legs. They had put up with Bear Growl for a long time. They had even talked about doing him in after he had passed out on one of his drunks. They felt he would be easier to live with after this. Or, they would have to band together and get rid of him themselves. The tall man showed them that Bear Growl was defeatable like the rest of them.

"He's not present tonight?" asked Milton.

"He's at the shack. He got one gawdawful head-hurt. He said to tell ya if'n we saw ya that he hopes ya fall off ya hoss an' breaks ya neck." Jackknife laughed.

There was more laughter.

"I thank him kindly for the wish of luck," Milton told them with a bow.

Plunder and Plug walked past.

Plug stopped and asked Milton, "Where's thet damned squaw?"

Milton did not bother to answer.

"Thet damned red bitch could be makin' us some money," growled Plug.

"Did ya leave her at the shack?" asked Plunder. As soon as he asked, he wished he had kept his mouth shut.

"I ain't the keeper of your woman an' I ain't a damned pimp. So, by God, don't ask me no more," Milton barked.

"Wal, we done let ya eat at our fire an' are lookin' after ya. There could be some friendliness there," complained Plug.

Milton turned to face Plug. His eyes could not be seen in the dark, but there was no doubt as to what he was thinking. One more crack by Mister Plug's tongue and it might get cut off.

"Come on, Plug. I done seed us a keg of rum for the askin'," Plunder said, leading his partner away.

The two men left, Plug stomping off with a sour look on his face.

"I just don' like that mon," Scotty said with a twisted mouth.

"I don' like either one of 'em. Thet Plunder laughs, but ya know he'll still be laughin' when he takes the pennies off'n yore eyes," Rover said without humor.

"Yeah, an' Plug beats on that Injun woman somethin' fierce. I wouldn't beat on a nigger like thet," Jackknife informed them.

"I gotta pee, boys. I held off as long as I could," Rover said, hating the job.

"He having problems?" asked Milton.

"Yeah, he's got one of them female diseases. Hit burns like hell when ya pee," Crip told him.

"All of us has it, mon, and it's called a venereal disease," Scotty informed Milton.

"Yeah, an little buggers thet crawl all over yer balls," Jackknife complained.

"I think I'll walk around and see what I can see," Milton told the men, moving on.

"Wonder who he be lookin' fer?" asked Crip.

"I don't know. Jest shore glad it ain't me," said a happy Jesse.

"That is a fact," Scotty agreed.

"Think he's the law?" asked Crip.

"Could be. Or he could be jest somebody out to settle a score. He looks the type that'd hate a long spell. But he ain't lookin' fer none of us, 'cause he's still a-lookin'."

"Thet shore relieves me some. I'd hate for thet tall feller to single me outta the herd," sighed Crip.

"That's fer a fact," agreed all of them.

* * *

Milton walked around the open dance ground. He did not know what he was looking for, just looking. He was sure of one thing. He was looking on one of the lower rungs of society.

He stood and watched the dancers in the flickering torchlight on the dance floor. Their antics were vulgar at times and merely hilarious at other times.

Sodom and Gomorrah right here in the swamps of the Neutral Strip!

He kept a wary eye out for any hostility that may be directed toward him. He wasn't exactly among friends.

Chapter Seventeen

One of the huge bodyguards of Big Red stepped to Milton's side. It was Lion Jaw. He growled, "Big Red want to see ya."

Milton looked from the dance floor and met Lion Jaw's eyes in the flickering torch light. Lion Jaw was one of the many in this camp who was lacking in advanced mentality, but unlike the others, he had power on his side. This made him dangerous.

"If he can walk, tell him I'd be pleased to see him," Milton said in a mild manner. *Strike now,* an inner voice told him.

Lion Jaw looked at Milton steadily. No, this man was not the bravado type who only did battle with his tongue. This man meant what he said, and he was not used to bowing to others' will. He would resist, which meant Lion Jaw would get the pleasure of cutting Mr. Tall One down to natural size.

"Ya want me to tell him thet?" Lion Jaw growled, still not sure that anyone would actually want to rebel against Big Red's authority.

"Word for word," Milton told him. "That is, if you can remember that long."

Anger flashed in Lion Jaw's eyes. But he knew he could not do anything until Big Red gave him the word. "Ya know, feller, me an' Tiny'll git in the last word."

Milton ignored him and turned back to the dancers.

Lion Jaw left with an outward scowl on his face, but a smile in his heart. Big Red would order him to bring the tall, uppity man over any way he had to. He knew exactly how he and Tiny were going to go about that pleasurable job.

"Mister, ya mighta bit off a bigger chunk than ya can chaw," a man standing next to Milton said.

Milton shrugged his shoulders. "Naw, I don't reckon I did."

"I shore hope ya got a small army hid out in the woods. Them two giants is not only big, they is downright animal by nature. They don' do nothin' fair."

It seemed that no one in camp liked Big Red and his gang.

"Who said I was fair?" asked Milton lightly. "How many besides those two?"

"Jest those two in camp right now. But they's five more outta the camp," the man told him. "Those five should be back tonight or tomorrow, so's I hear."

"How 'bout Red?" asked Milton.

"If you git past those two, which ain't likely, Big Red's got a brace of pistols to finish the talk with. An' let me tell ya, he's an expert wit' those two things. Best pistol shot I ever seed," the man informed him. "Thet li'l feller won't hesitate to shoot anybody thet'd question his leadership of this camp. He kilt his favorite cousin a few months back."

"Nice family you got runnin' this camp," Milton commented.

"Yep, they is," the man admitted.

"The rest of the camp with him an' his crew?" asked Milton, looking around for Lion Jaw and Tiny to return.

"Nope. We jest ain't got no other choice," the man replied. He looked around him to make sure no one could overhear. "Ain't no one group thet kin get a leader everybody agrees wit'. Arguin'est bunch of critters I ever seed. Can't agree on nary a thing. Course, Big Red keeps rumors goin' to keep everybody split up. Smart, ain't he?"

Milton didn't agree on the smart part, but he knew how groups like this operated. One group with a leader was organized enough to gain control and the rest sat around and complained about their lack of organization. But he had a chance if the rest of the camp would like to see Big Red lose control. If he took out Big Red, the rest of a grateful camp would allow him a chance to escape from this place. He made up his mind. As usual, he didn't waste time thinking about it. He knew what he had to do.

"Here comes Lion Jaw an' he's got Tiny wit' him," the man said in a low voice. He beat a hasty retreat from Milton's side.

Milton sang his war song to himself.

"Feller, Big Red said he don' walk over to no one," Lion Jaw informed Milton with a smile.

Everyone stepped back from Milton, as if he'd suddenly broken out with the pox.

"Is that a fact," Milton said over the loud music that had suddenly broken out, a Highland fling. "Then I reckon we can't have our little chat."

"Big Red said we could bring ya any way we could git you thar," Lion Jaw told him happily. "So you gotta walk it on yore own, or if'n we carry ya, it'll be a one-way trip."

"Boys, ya lay one of your shit-grabbers on this child an' ya just might draw back a nub," Milton told them in his mild-mannered tone of voice.

The two men looked at each other. They were not used to being opposed. At least, not openly.

"Wal, gawddamn it to hell, I done lost my patience!" Lion Jaw bellowed. Milton let the man get close enough to him for Lion Jaw to grab him by the arm. In one fluid motion Milton pulled his tomahawk and slashed Lion Jaw on the elbow, nearly cutting the arm in two. His second blow found Lion Jaw's carotid artery and jugular vein on the left side of his bull-sized neck. The giant of a man dropped to the ground, dead as he fell.

Tiny was slow. He was pulling his pistol when Milton's war ax bit deeply into his skull, seeking his "seat of life." Tiny dropped without a sound, dead as he hit the ground.

The dance broke up and the music ground to a halt. A quiet suddenly fell over the happy throng. Sudden death will sometimes affect even the most hardened.

A high-pitched scream pierced the night air. The dance

ground emptied, leaving an opening between Milton and Big Red.

"You! You! Attack my men, will ye?" screamed Big Red, running toward Milton.

Without a word or pause Milton threw his tomahawk. It covered the twenty-one paces that divided them in a split second. The blade buried itself deep in Big Red's forehead. His hands had reached his pistol butts, but he had not drawn them: the outlaw leader should have been shooting instead of shouting.

The crowd gasped. This was something all of them had dreamed and hoped for, but none had ever thought possible. An uneasy cheer went up.

"Man, ya came for business, didn't ya?" the man who had stood beside him asked a stated question.

"I didn't come here to talk," Milton said bluntly. He had drawn his knife and stood ready to react to attack from any direction.

"No need to worry about others," a man told him. "We'uns is gonna leave you be."

"Jest lookit! By Gawd, he kilt Big Red!"

"An' both his two animals!"

There was joy in their voices.

"Ya jest made yoreself a passel of frien's, tall man."

"Yeah, but ye gotta leave. Red's got a nephew an' four others thet'll do ye in on a spit if they's catched ye."

The "Big" was already being dropped from the name.

"They'll spit ya over a slow burnin' fire."

Milton walked over to Big Red and withdrew his tomahawk with a firm jerk. He used Big Red's shirt to wipe the weapon clean.

"Did ye seen thet tomahawk fly?"

"Gawd, yes."

"Ain't no Injun coulda done better," an admirer said.

"Wonder if'n he wuz raised by Injuns."

"Come to think on it, those are Cherokee moccasins he's a-wearin'. High tops they's called—'shoe-boots.'"

"Hell, I got Injun moccasins, an' I weren't raised by no Injuns!"

The men agreed. Talk came after battles, sex, and booze. They hadn't done any fighting, but they had seen some quick, furious battle on this night. It loosed the tongue.

"Them Cherokees ain't heatherns like them others. He couldn'ta been raised by them. They's civilized Injuns."

"Thet's right, they ain't got warriors lak them Shawnee."

"You two are as ignert as they comes on facts 'bout redskins. Jest who the hell do ya think kept them Shanee an' everybody else run outa Kentuck?"

Milton looked around at the people on the edges of the dance ground. He caught Plug's eyes in the soft glow of the light and held it for a moment. Plug broke contact and his eyes fell.

"Ya'd better saddle up an' ride outta here, mister. Ya ain't got none of us to worry about, but when thet nephew of Red's gets back, all hell is gonna break loose. Like somebody done said, they's five of 'em."

"Ride on outta here. Nobody's gonna stop ye."

Here was his chance. They were offering him a way out, free and clear.

Jesse, Scotty, and Crip broke through the ranks.

"Tall 'Un, git on thet hoss of our'n an' ride," Jesse urged him. "They's too many of them guys an' ain't nobody gonna help ye here."

Milton didn't say another word, but wheeled and strode out of the firelight.

"So long, Tall 'Un," Jesse called.

Milton went directly to the lean-to.

Morning Light stood beside a saddled horse. His pony was saddled and his gear tied to the back of the saddle.

"That hoss don't take kindly to other people," he told her.

"He ain't so mean," she said simply. "I been kicked around by men. No damn horse is going to do the same."

He laughed and took his rifle from her. "You knew it would be tonight?"

"I had a dream. I dreamed a tall, dark man would come to take me to my people. You are here. You are not the type to take long to do something," she told him simply.

Indians and their dreams. He said in English, "Stop talkin' an' let's do some ridin'."

"I know we will escape this evil place. My dreams say it will be so," she told him confidently.

They mounted and rode through the camp. Milton led south, down a trail that cut through the center of the camp.

"Hey, somebody's wit' him!" someone called.

"Who?" another asked.

"Gawddammit to hell! I bet the sonofabitch's got our squaw!" cried Plug.

"Fergit thet damned squaw!" urged Plunder.

"Fergit, hell, thet's money riding off there, Plunder!" Then it dawned on Plug that something else was leaving. "An' she's got one of our hosses! Thet red bitch has stole one of our hosses!"

"Hell, Plug, we can git us'n 'nother squaw. An' we kin git us'n 'nother hoss. But we don' need to git us no kind of thet trouble ridin' there," Plunder reminded him.

"I want my property back! Somebody go wit' me!" yelled Plug.

Men laughed.

"Got his squaw!" laughed Jackknife.

"Go git him, squaw man. But ya git him by yoreself," laughed Jesse.

"I ain't ridin' nowhere, no time, after thet big man," Crip told them.

"He's broke the code! Our code! He stole from a camp member!" Plug reminded them.

"He ain't broke my code," a man called.

"He ain't took no oath on nothin'." Jesse laughed.

"He might not be no regular outlaw," another one said.

"What do ya thunk he might be?"

"I don't know an' I ain't gonna ask." said Jesse.

"Ya damned cowards! If'n thet be yore propity, I'd go wit ya to git it back." Plug was nearly sobbing.

"Plug, you is a case." Plunder shook his head and walked off.

"Let's git these bodies outta here an' git this shindig back on the road!"

Plug stood, gazing into the dark as if he would be able to catch a glimpse of his vanishing property.

After they'd cleared camp, Milton stopped his horse in the middle of the trail and stepped down. He took off his broad-brimmed hat and tied it to his saddle. His buckskin hat and pants joined his hat. He stood a few moments with his eyes closed, as he had been taught by his old Cherokee teachers, letting his being join with nature around him. He stood motionless to get himself as one with the darkness and the forest, singing a song of the forest. Milton mentally prepared himself to "set the pace of a warrior." Then, he would be able to run hour after hour on the dark trail, not a tree branch or even a leaf touching him. Total darkness or sudden blindness would not deter him. He would be able to "see" all things around him by other means.

Without a word he started forward at a dogtrot. His "eyes" would be searching for the third trail that led to his right.

The pony followed along behind him as it had been taught.

Morning Light didn't know why they had stopped. She had heard that Cherokees were more comfortable on foot when in strange territory.

Milton ran, dodging tree limbs and making turns he could not see with normal vision. He used every sense in his naked body to see his surroundings. It was one of the things he had learned to do as a young boy.

When he came to the first and second trails, he bypassed

them. He had not seen them with his eyes, yet he knew they were there.

He ran tirelessly, mile after mile, hour after hour. A fine mist cooled his face as he ran. The two horses followed at a trot. Unseen tree limbs slapped and tugged at Morning Light. The ride became a nightmare to her. One thing kept her going: the thought of getting back to her people. For that she could run through cactus naked.

The third trail came up and Milton automatically turned down it. He ran until he reached the Sabine River, two and one half hours before daylight. He walked to the river's edge, knelt, and drank deeply. The river was swollen by the spring rains and tasted of mud and debris.

They quickly made a cold camp, working without words to slow their progress. When their bedrolls were in place and their horses taken care of, Milton took a quick dip in the river. Morning Light was snoring by the time he returned to the fireless camp. He was anxious for some sleep and rest himself.

Chapter Eighteen

Milton woke just before dawn. Morning Light sat up. The deep blackness that comes just before dawn held them in the palm of their own world. Their world was wet with heavy dew. Fog rolled from the river and onto the surrounding banks, cutting off visibility even more.

"You didn't sit up to guard me all night," she complained in a mocking voice. "Plug might have come after me."

"We had a guard," Milton told her.

"Oh?" a questioning sound in her voice.

"Him," Milton told her, jerking his thumb toward his horse. She could not see his gesture. "Him, who?"

"That old Plains Indian pony of mine," Milton informed her. "The best guard horse you ever saw."

She sat a moment and then put on her blouse. "I would let you play, tall man, but I have a sickness."

"A bad one?" he asked, wondering what could be all that bad.

"The worst." There was sadness in her voice.

"Is it catching?" he asked, wondering what he had gotten himself into.

"Only for those who crawl between my blankets," she assured him.

"Did the men in the camp know?" he could not help but ask.

"No, they did not know. That is the reason I like to go from blanket to blanket," she told him in a terse voice.

Milton laughed. He laughed heartily. This was the kind of humor and justice he understood. No wonder the men were

going around scratching themselves and holding on to a tree
to keep running off every time they relieved themselves.

"When the disease eats off their noses, I would like to be
there to tell them that it was I, Morning Light, the dirty Injun
squaw, who gave it to them." She laughed without humor.

Milton laughed again, bending over to his knees in his
mirth.

"They gave it to me. Was it not my duty to spread it
around?" she asked.

Milton continued to laugh on his way to his morning ritual
of "going to water."

Morning Light also came for her morning bath and to greet
the new sun in the Quapaw way. It did not bother Morning
Light for Milton to see her naked body. They were Indians,
and they did not have vulgar thoughts about things that are
normal acts, like taking a bath.

Milton knew that there would be Neutral Strip outlaws
coming after him. A delegation from the first camp would
reach the second camp by this morning. The words *Texas law*
would have most of the camp up in arms. The men had seen
him in action and would not want to follow him. But there
was Big Red's nephew and crew. He would have a few follow-
ers who would come along to try and get next to the new
powers. He knew Plug would drag Plunder along to be among
the group to come after Milton. With all of that behind him,
he had just as soon be in Texas.

After a quick breakfast of jerked meat and corn mush
washed down with hot coffee, Milton found a desirable river
crossing. The rain-widened river ran swift, but they managed
to cross to the far bank without mishap.

The thirty-five-mile ride to Devil's Diggings was a time-
consuming, uneventful trip. They rode through the community of scattered houses of Devil's Diggings, then across the
Neches River and on to Captain Stephen Prather's Indian
trading post.

When they reached the trading post, Milton stepped down

from his tired horse. Two Alabama Indian men watched him as he went into the building, followed by Morning Light.

"Wal, I'll declare, if'n it ain't Mr. Milton Hicks in person," Stephen Prather said when he saw them. "Thet yore new ridin' wife, Panther Killer?"

"No, I picked her up travelin'," Milton told him with a smile, glad to see Prather. "How do, Cap'n?"

"Jest fine, Milton, jest fine," the handsome man told him.

The two men shook hands as men will do who do not get to see each other often. They had known each other for a number of years. Their friendship was not close, but it was the kind that would endure as long as they lived. It was the kind of friendship in which one might call upon the other in time of need, when the going got rough.

"Where ye been travelin', Milton? Ye look traveled out. So does the lady with you," observed Stephen.

" 'Cross the Sabine in the ole' Neutral Strip. Lookin' for somebody," Milton told him.

"Ye be in those camps?" asked Stephen, knowing Milton was one of the few who would try such a thing.

"Yep. Got through all of 'em," Milton said lightly. He cut off a couple of slices of cheese, handing some to Morning Light.

"Ye musta wanted him bad like," Prather commented, looking the woman over. He did not ask Milton whom he was looking for. Milton would eventually get around to that.

"This is Morning Light. She is a Quapaw woman," Milton said. "A couple of them Strip outlaws kidnapped her an' passed her around. She be their source of income when they couldn't take it stealin'. She has been used sorely."

"The sorry bastards! Nothin' but white trash, all of 'em over there," spat Stephen Prather, the warrior's blood creeping to his neck. "Give me a couple hundert Indian warriors an' I'd clean thet bunch out. Them army boys over in the States ain't ever gonna git it done."

"Yeah, I know. There are other women in there thet needs

to be got out," Milton informed him. "I seen some of 'em.
They's black wimmin, along with Indian and white. They'd
rather have all white or black wimmin. Them Indian wimmin
won't become slaves an' just won't gee an' haw like they're
supposed to."

An Indian was of no use to anyone in captivity to be used as
a slave. If sold in bondage, most would quit living and soon
died. A red man was of value to none but himself.

"Can you see that she gets to her people?" asked Milton.

"Shore. A group of Quapaws moved up north of the Cherokees, on the Red River. Maybe it's some of her people," said
Stephen. Then he asked, "She been with them outlaws long?"

" 'Bout three or four year, she tells me," Milton said, ac-
cepting the mug of beer. He gulped it down in his thirst.

Stephen handed a mug to Morning Light. To hell with the
law against selling alcohol to Indians. She deserved one beer.
But she turned it down and indicated she wanted water.

"She told me that the only thing that kept her going was her
dreams. She believed a tall, dark man would come and rescue
her, taking her back to her people," Milton told Stephen. "She
tried to escape a number of times. Just got the hell beat outta
her for her efforts. But after the dreams she gave up trying to
escape."

"Wal, ye be the tall, dark stranger. Ye are Indian enough to
know never doubt an Indian's dream," Stephen reminded
him.

"Reckon yo're right," Milton agreed. "My ole granddaddy
always tole me to stop wondering an' keep believing."

"How do ye talk to her?" asked Stephen.

"I use Choctaw trade language," Milton told him. He
quickly finished the beer and Stephen dipped him another
one.

Stephen was an old trader among the Indians. He could
speak both Choctaw and Caddo.

"There's a Coushatta woman here who will take care of
her," Prather told Milton. Then he told the woman using

Choctaw, "Go to the back of the building. You will find a Coushatta woman making soap."

Morning Light looked at Milton. He nodded his head that it was all right.

"White man, this tall breed man is a great warrior," Morning Light told Stephen. "He killed the camp chief, Big Red, and his two giants. Then he take me from there. This Quapaw woman will always remember."

She said her little piece and left.

"Ye still hittin' them guys without talkin' about it?" asked Stephen with a grin.

"A man either fights or he talks about it. Talking wastes time an' doesn't get the job done," Milton said simply. Then he asked, "You seen Thumping Turtle lately?"

"Ah, so that's who ye be after! I heard about the trouble he'd be in. But I hadn't heard ye be after him." Stephen laughed.

"Bean."

"Ole' Pete sent you, huh? He takes great store in yore abilities. Said the onliest thing thet kept ye from bein' a leader was thet ye jest don't cotton to society too much."

He stopped long enough to "Howdy" people coming in. One of his clerks got a workout while he talked to an old friend. Now that the woman had left, it was time to talk.

"When I got things to do, I want to do 'em. I don't want to have to ask nobody for permission to have a little time off," Milton said bluntly.

"Yeah, Milton, Thumpin' Turtle's been through here," Stephen told him. "I was gone an' didn't git back 'till last night. They tole me thet he left yesterday mornin', sayin' he had been away from home too long."

Milton knew that if Prather had been there, Thumping Turtle would have stayed. Milton wanted to know, "He drunked up?"

"They tell me he was as sober as a newborn babe still on the tit. Didn't take none with him either," said Stephen, offering Milton another beer.

Milton turned it down.

Stephen continued, "It seems Turtle don't know ye be after him."

"He will now. He'll get the word," Milton assured him.

"It's gonna be one hell of a fight," Stephen said, to himself as much as to Milton.

"Yep, I reckon," Milton said modestly.

"By, God, Milton, ye are really wantin' this un, don' ye?" exclaimed Stephen.

"He's a woman beater. He's done it many times when he gets likkered up. It's a bad habit an' I ain't gonna stand by an' watch it when I can do something about it," Milton said bluntly.

"You can't right all the wrongs," Stephen informed him.

"Don't reckon. But I will those I can."

Milton walked over and cut another slice of cheese from the large block on the counter.

"Thumpin' Turtle has give his people a lot of trouble. He's one hell of a warrior, but he's still trouble. Ole' Long King has had about a bellyful of him. He's gonna be rough to take, but of course, ye already know thet," said Stephen.

"He can be taken."

"Nobody has yet."

"Milton Hicks ain't tried yet," Milton said in a matter-of-fact voice.

"Yep, reckon yo're right," Stephen agreed. "Milton, stay the night an' go in the mornin'. We got plenty of campin' spots 'round here."

"Thanks, Cap'n, I'll do that." He was also thinking about five or more others who might be following him. He would just as soon face them here.

"How be things in Nacogdoches and area?" asked Stephen. He wasn't finished talking and would keep Milton busy at it until he had finished. Or the breed up and walked out on him. Milton was capable of doing that, and not thinking he was being impolite either.

"Changing, yet staying the same. You know how Texas be. Things never change, yet things change continuously," Milton told him.

"How's the cocky li'l colonel, Piedras? Thet sawed-off li'l bastard still runnin' scared about Anglos comin' in?" Stephen wanted to know. He knew Piedras well and thought he was a real pain.

"Yeah, he's nervous as hell. Sees a conspiracy behind every tree. One in every gathering of Anglos. Our li'l ole colonel is goin' to *la casa de locos.*" Milton smiled.

"He does act the lunatic sometimes. He's gonna cause this part of Mexico a lot of trouble 'afore it's over with. He's the type," complained Stephen. He was another one who kept up on the political situation of the country.

"I don't reckon it'll affect me none. Jest let me ride an' look this ole' world over, that's all I ask. I'll let everybody else do their own thing in their own way," Milton told him. He handed a list to the man behind the counter. He was ready to break off the conversation.

"Things don't work out like thet in this ole' world, Milton," Stephen reminded him.

"Yeah, I know it's the dream of us foot loose an' fancy-free types. But, hell, Stephen, even you rooted-down individuals got dreams," Milton reminded him. "If'n you didn't, what you buildin' this store up for?"

"Each to his own, I reckon." He knew the tall breed had talked all he was going to. He would let him go.

Get roots, stay in one place, live long, and die badly, thought Milton. That was not the kind of life for him.

Milton picked up the items he had bought and walked out to his horse. He led him to the banks of the small tributary that led into the Neches River. He unsaddled his pony, talking to him. He spoke in Spanish. "Hey, little four-legged brother, so you let a woman get hold of you and subdue you, huh?"

The horse flopped his ears a couple of times, then lowered them to say he was not much interested in conversation.

Milton smiled. He, too, knew when someone had had enough talk. He hobbled the horse's front legs so he could graze and go to the stream for water.

Milton still felt no one was going to steal this wild pony. Not unless they had Morning Light with them.

Chapter Nineteen

Morning Light was at his camp when he came from the river at dawn. A small fire was burning. The smoke curled lazily up to mingle and get lost in the heavy fog. Beside the fire was a plate of pork, corn grits, and fry bread. His uncle had told him to never eat pig meat. A man was what he ate and a warrior should never partake of the meat of any slow, sluggish animal. But Milton lived in a white world. He ate what was available.

"There is talk. They say the man you seek is a great warrior. They say that he will not run. They say that you will kill him. They say that it will not be easy," she informed him.

He smiled at her. "They say?"

"They" were the people of the community. People she did not know, but her people for the night.

"Do you know of this man?" she wanted to know.

"I know him," he told her, digging into the food.

"Is he a great warrior like they say?" she asked.

"He is known to be such. I reckon I'll find out."

"So, that's it! The greater the warrior, the greater the glory," she said, understanding. "You know, you will never be completely white."

"So be it. I have never asked that it not be so." He held out his cup for a refill. He was glad the coffee had no chicory.

"Do these Spanish let you be Indian and white?" she asked, not sure she could believe such a thing.

"Yes, the Spanish did, and now it's the Mexicans. That is their way," he informed her.

"And yet they are white people?" she asked.

"Some of them are. Most Mexican are Indian or breeds," he

said, reaching for some more bread. "Most of the men in high office of the government are white."

"Most of these Mexicans are red men, yet they live like white men," she said, shaking her head with incomprehension.

"Soon you will be back with your people. Captain Prather will see to it. He is a good man. I have known him for many years," Milton told her.

"If you say so, I believe it," she said gratefully, "I wish I didn't have this sickness so I could show you how I feel."

"You don't need to," Milton said. "I know."

"I will remember my dream and the tall, dark man who came for me."

There was nothing more for them to say.

He finished his meal. He did not thank her. Most Indians do not give thanks or accept thanks for something done. If an Indian wished to do something for a person, he did so gladly. So why should thanks be given or received for something gladly done?

He broke camp and, after saddling his horse, rode to the front of the trading post. Morning Light walked beside the horse.

As he rounded the corner of the building, he saw them. Seven men rode out of the morning fog; the soft glow of the new sun trying to break through the mist was at their backs. Milton knew who they would be. Plug, Plunder, Big Red's nephew and gang. There had been sixteen of them at the start. Four of them had refused to cross the Sabine River into Mexico. Five more had refused to go past Devil's Diggings, feeling that they had come too far into Texas.

Milton rode to the front of the trading post and turned his horse to face the oncoming men. The new position took the sun from the backs of the men. The sun was no problem at the moment, but who knew when it might burn itself through the thinly veiled haze.

Stephen Prather came out of the building, his long rifle in his hands. A white man and three red men walked from behind a small building to Milton's right. All four were armed and out of sight of the men on horseback.

"I figured ye jest might have stirred up more trouble than would stay laid," Prather called to Milton. "We be waitin'. We be ready."

Milton nodded.

Five more guns cut down the odds.

"Come on inside, Morning Light," Stephen told her.

"I stay," she informed him, ending the conversation.

The man leading the group was a young man in his mid-twenties with shoulder-length reddish-gold hair. Milton could see his arrogance even from this distance.

The men fanned out as they got closer. They stopped about one hundred and fifty feet from Milton. They had been told about his tomahawk.

The two groups of men spent a short amount of time looking and measuring each other. The situation was dangerous. A man who led a normal life could live out his existence and never be in this kind of situation. These men did not lead normal lives. But even for men such as these, it was not an everyday occurrence.

The smell of death hung heavy with the fog. The stench of nervous fear mixed with the smell of woodsmoke and cooked food was thick in each man's nostrils.

"Thet be the man?" the blond asked.

"Thet be him, Brute," Plunder answered.

Brute was larger than his uncle had been, but he was far from being a giant. It seemed that a strong vein of overly expanded self-esteem ran very high in the family.

"An' thar's our woman," Plug added. "Whar's our hoss, woman?"

"Tall man, we come to settle with ye. Thet was my uncle you murdered back thar," Brute cried out his anger.

"An' we want our woman an' hoss back too," put in Plug.

"Gawddamnit, Plug, shet up 'bout thet damned squaw!" Brute spat.

"Thet's money on the hoof, Brute," Plunder dared put in.

"I'm gonna shoot thet bitch right here an' now, then we'll see who wants her after thet," growled Brute.

Plunder kept quiet, sitting slumped in the saddle. Plug had a mean snarl on his face, but he kept his mouth in check.

"We aim to do to ye what ye did to Big Red," Brute threatened Milton. "Ye was armed to the hilt an' done them in. They didn' have a chance. But we air ready for ye. Ye ain't gonna catch us off guard."

"If you're gonna do it, get with it. I got things to do," Milton barked at him.

The response threw Brute off. Here was a man facing seven assailants with only one other man to back him up, on the verge of getting himself killed, and he showed no sign of nervousness. There was only impatience because he was being inconvenienced!

"Thet wuz my uncle ye killed!" yelled Brute.

And I'm gonna kill his nephew. Milton raised his rifle, took quick aim, and fired. Before the bullet struck Brute in the chest, Milton dug his heels into his horse's sides, drawing his tomahawk as he rode. The Indian war pony charged straight for the targets his master had pointed him to. He would place his rider in the position where he would be most effective, and that was right in the middle of them.

Milton's rifle ball hit Brute in the breastbone, and plowed through his chest, driving splintered bone into his heart and lungs before shattering his backbone on the way out. Brute would seek no more vengeance for his uncle.

Two more men fell before he reached the group. Rifle fire from the four men on his right flank caught the outlaws off guard. One of the fallen men was Plunder. A third man was felled by Stephen's rifle fire.

Stephen and his men could no longer safely fire, with Milton in the center of the group of outlaws.

Milton let go with a fierce war cry as he reached his first target. He swung his tomahawk at a ducking man. The razor-sharp blade took off the top of the man's head, his brains splattering over the victim and his horse.

The war pony never paused, but jumped straight for the next horse and rider, running over them, knocking both to the ground. Milton's horse stumbled but kept its feet. The man screamed as Milton's horse bit off his left ear and part of his face.

Milton wheeled his horse and sank his tomahawk into the head of the injured man, cutting short his scream. The horse wheeled, both man and beast searching for the next adversary.

Plug was the only one on his horse. He held his long pistol in his hand. "Looks lak yore friens air still tryin' to load, tall man. I'm gonna blow ya in two."

A look of surprise dropped over Plug's face as a shot sounded and the bullet passed through his body. Without a word his lifeless body slipped from the dying horse to the ground.

"You always did talk too much," Milton told Plug, and then spit in his face. That was for his horse.

Stephen walked up to Milton. "I always keep an extra rifle handy."

"That's why you're the captain," Milton told him with a slight smile.

"What was he shootin' off his mouth about?" asked Stephen, reloading his rifle.

"Tellin' me how mean he was," Milton stated dryly.

"He should of shot off thet pistol. Yes, suh, it don't pay to talk too much sometimes," laughed Stephen, swatting at the late-morning mosquitoes.

"It shore don't most of the time," agreed Milton. " 'Specially when ya go round talkin' 'bout killin' somebody."

"This wuz a talkin' bunch, all right. Ye reckon they had much time to do any outlawyin'?" Stephen asked, looking them over. "I ain't even seen any of this bunch round here 'afore."

"They musta done something." Milton shrugged.

Morning Light walked up to Plug and kicked him. She looked at Milton. He nodded his head, indicating that she could do as she wished. She pulled Plug's knife out of his belt and took his scalp. She went next to Plunder and started cutting him.

Plunder groaned. As the knife cut deeper, a gurgling wail escaped from the tortured man.

Morning Light did not pause. She cut a circle around his scalp lock, deliberately placed a foot on his face, covering his mouth, and gave a sharp tug. The scalp came loose with a ripping sound.

A muffled scream came from the semiconscious Plunder.

Morning Light stuck the knife in the ground next to Plunder's head. She told Milton, "When I get back to my people, I will dance many times over these scalps in memory of this day."

The Quapaw woman walked off with the two scalps, a look of victory and pride on her face.

"She wuz downright mad at those two, weren't she?" Stephen asked unnecessarily.

"That be them, or what's left of 'em, that treated her so sorely." Milton kicked his horse over to where Plunder lay. He pulled out his long horse-pistol and fired. The bullet went through the outlaw's mutilated head.

Plunder's body gave an involuntary jump, then lay quiet.

"Got yore scalp took with yore own knife," commented Stephen on Plug's misfortune. "I tell ye, Milton, I been killin' an' takin' scalps all my life. Seen it done, too, many times. But it do give me a quiver to see an Indian take a white man's scalp."

Milton made no comment on that. There was no need to. That was the way it was and he could not change it. It did not make him feel any the worse because his friend differentiated that way between white men and red men. He would live and die with that difference riding with him, as it had all of his life.

He reloaded both his weapons.

Stephen called to the white man and three red men. "Let's

see if anybody knows this scum. Might be some bounty money. Then git them buried. It's gonna git hot 'afore long an' them bodies'll be stinkin' somethin' awful!"

The men came forward to perform their duty. The outlaws were stripped of all their valuables before they were carried off. These were practical men of the frontier.

"Ye know, don't ye, thet the next one ain't gonna be so easy," Stephen reminded Milton.

"I don't reckon," Milton admitted.

"He'll want Indian justice. He'll ask for a fight with knife or tomahawk, Milton."

"Good choice."

Stephen wanted to go along, bad. But there were times a man did things alone and others did not try to intrude. His friend Milton Hicks did most things alone.

"Tell ole' Pete Bean to come by," Stephen told Milton.

"Will do."

"An' ole Long King. Tell him I got them seeds," Stephen remembered.

"I'll tell him."

Milton rode out, lifting a hand to all. He pulled up his horse in front of Morning Light for a moment.

"Ride with care, tall man. You ride dangerous trails," she told him.

He kicked his horse onto the trail leading north.

Chapter Twenty

He rode on the trail, a narrow path wide enough for carts to travel, that followed along the west bank of the Neches River. He would ride this trail until he came to a trail leading west and to the Coushatta town.

It was impossible to ride across the forest between the Neches and Trinity rivers. The only passages through the thick vegetation were the many animal trails that crisscrossed the big thicket area. But only those who hunted this area regularly would dare venture down the maze of trails. To keep from being lost forever, everyone else was forced to travel on the well-defined trails between red and white settlements.

The trail ran from Devil's Diggings to the small village of Teran. The trail had dried some over the past few days, but it was still muddy and nearly impassable to wheeled vehicles.

Immediately after that though, he heard the squeaking of the carreta, a Spanish two-wheeled cart, coming from the direction of Teran. The cart had wooden wheels that usually went ungreased and shrieked with every revolution. This cart was no different from the rest. The cart was pulled by four oxen plodding along with no sign of effort pulling their load of wood. The two Mexican men doffed their large sombreros to Milton as they passed. That was the only traffic he met on that trail.

Before reaching Teran, Milton found the well-worn trail used by the Coushatta Indians to go back and forth to Prather's Indian trading post. He and his stout little warhorse faced a hundred miles to the Coushatta town on the banks of the Trinity River. It would be midmorning the following day before they would reach their destination. He met only two Coushatta men on this trail during the entire day. Not many were willing to travel this boggy route with all the rivers, creeks, and other waterways at flood stage.

Milton found a small stream of water to make his evening camp among the thick vegetation of many different kinds of soft woods and hard woods, among them different species of pine and oak. There was also magnolia, sweet gum, red gum, hackberry, and dozens of different species of fruit trees. There were enough different types of trees to keep any carpenter or furniture maker happy for the rest of his life. The undergrowth was nearly impassable because of thick growths of berries and other vine plants, loaded with thorns.

His night was spent quietly, free of people, as he liked it.

His only visitors were the animals of the forest. They came in the late evening light to stare at him in wonder. Today it was he who was the strange-looking creature in the forest.

He remembered all the animal stories and traditional stories his Cherokee teachers had taught him in his youth. The Cherokee teachers had been more interesting to him than the white teachers. Rich Joe Vann had hired the first white missionaries to come and teach the family children. Elizabeth, the only sister of Milton's grandfather, Chief Charles Hicks, had been married to Rich Joe Vann at one time. Some of the Vann children were his cousins.

But these white teachers who came to the Cherokee Nation, both those hired by individual families and the Nation, were stern, cheerless men who only taught. They never shared themselves with their students or allowed the children to share their knowledge with them. They also had a habit of trying to give corporal punishment to the Cherokee children. More than one white teacher had left the Cherokee Nation in haste with some angry father or mother in hot pursuit, the white teacher having insulted one of his young charges.

Milton was fortunate to have been taught by his grandfather, the old chief, long before the coming of the Christian

missionary teachers. Milton's grandfather had many white
men's books, and he had enjoyed the white men's history
books at first. But when he began to see a pattern of slavery
and complete submission of conquered countries and peoples
by nation after nation over the centuries, he lost interest.

He enjoyed his red teacher who taught him how to survive
in the real world of today. During this learning phase he was
taught about the animals of the forest and their relationship to
man. He was told that man could at one time, long, long ago,
talk to animals, for they all had the same language. Man even
talked to plants and insects, for all living creatures had the
same language. As usual, the stupidity of man destroyed even
that, so Asgaya Galulati, Man Above, the Great Creator of all
things, changed everyone's language and man could no longer
speak to the animals and plants.

These were his thoughts as he sat near his small campfire.
And while he thought thoughts of his early childhood teach-
ings, some of the animals of his youth paraded to his camp,
looked, and departed. Some of them even gave small perfor-
mances for his benefit. Like the two *kuli*, as raccoons are called
by the Cherokees. They put on a tumbling act for him. They
both wore masks so they could go about the forest doing mischief and no one would know who they were. It was said that
the raccoon took off his mask only when at home and in the
presence of his own people.

Yanu, the bear, walked up to the campsite. He stood on his
hind legs, for he was now in the presence of man and wished
to show his close relation to the two-legged creature. They say
that the bears are transformed Cherokee who were once members of a clan called Ani-Tsaguhi. That was long ago. Their
chief is White Bear and their town house is at Kuwahi, the
Mulberry Place, near Clingman's Dome in the Great Smoky
Mountains. They say that when man is not around or when
the bears go into council, they walk about on their hind legs
and talk to each other just like men. Their towns are so well
hidden that no man has found one. The bears are protectors of

the enchanted lake of Atagahi, Gall Place, where bears go to cure their sicknesses and hurts. They discovered the lake and let all of their brother animals use it, but it is kept secret from man. Man would turn the enchanted place into a place of slaughter and filth. It is said that when some people become old and crabby, they go off into the woods to become bears. That is why they are never seen again.

Milton threw food to the bear. The bear ate his gift from the man and went back into the forest. Milton knew that the great animal would linger just outside his camp the rest of the night. Pity the man who tried to molest his provider.

Utsa nati, he-has-a-bell, the rattlesnake, crawled across the trail and into the forest on the far side. Milton did not believe all the stories of the red man any more than he did of the white man. But the rattlesnake was highly honored by the Cherokee and he had never killed one himself. Only the *adawehi*, religious leaders of the Cherokee, had the power to kill a rattlesnake and not have its spirit bother them.

The next animal hung by its tail, waiting for the darkness of night to come before going out roaming. Milton happened to see him in a distant tree when he looked up. *Sikwa*, taken from *utsetasti*, "he grins," the opossum, preferred the dark of night as his protection.

He smelled it before it got within sight. It was not *dili*, the skunk, but *sugi*, the mink. The Cherokees also called the onion *sugi* for obvious reasons. The mink smells so badly because of his punishment as a habitual thief by the other animals of the forest. *Sugi* was such a bad thief that the animals threw him in a fire and when they smelled roasted flesh, they thought he had been punished enough. The lesson did no good, for he is as much a thief today as he ever was. But at least he can be smelled and kept track of whenever he is around.

This tall man of two worlds sat and enjoyed watching the animals of the forest parade by. They seemed to understand that he was no threat to them. No thought entered his mind that he should kill one of these animals. A man did not kill just for the hell of it. This fact separated him from other men of his worlds.

It was a pleasant interlude for a man who was on his way to kill or be killed.

Chapter Twenty-one

The following morning, Milton rode into the Coushatta town on the east bank of the Trinity River.

The people of the town carried on with their everyday affairs. Corn was being ground to make bread, deer hides dressed from the winter kill were being used to make clothing, flint was being chipped into projectile points, a new deerhorn spoon was being made.

But Milton could feel the undercurrent of anxious hostility in the town. They knew who he was. They knew whom he had come after. He was coming after one of their own. The "Indian hunter" had arrived. It made little or no difference that the one he was after was a troublemaker in his own town and had been all his life. He had blood kin here. He had children and wives here. He was a well-known warrior of much bravery. He was one of them. Over four hundred pairs of eyes watched Milton ride in among them.

Milton did not fear riding into this village. They were not at war with him or the white man. And the red man had better manners than most when a stranger came into his midst. If the red man had not been so peaceful and generous with strangers, there would not be so many white men in what they called the Americas.

Milton rode to the lodge with the staff of the war chief outside the door. Long King, war chief of the Texas Coushatta, was the most powerful and important man of his people. His advanced age was not a deterrent to his performing the duties of war chief.

He stopped his horse in front of the lodge and remained

astride the animal. He had not been invited to step down from his mount. He waited patiently.

Long King came out of his lodge. His hair was shoulder length and white as snow. His body had shrunk with the long years, but he still stood straight and tall. "Ah, Tall One, you are here? We have been waiting for you."

"It is good to see the great war chief of the Coushatta people. Are you well, grandfather?" Milton inquired politely.

"Except for age, I am well, tall warrior. How is my friend, the old Bowl?" Long King wanted to know.

"The last time I saw him he was well," replied Milton.

"All of the old people who came with us from the land of our fathers will soon be dead. Then all will be gone and there will be no one to remember how it was in the old days," the old man complained. He was thinking about a lost home. Of a divided people. About a home of his youth that he would not see again before his death. Maybe his spirit would pass over the graves of his fathers before it passed from this world and into the afterlife.

Milton sat his horse, letting the old man carry the conversation.

"I hear my friend Bowl has another wife. It this true?" Long King asked with a smile.

"It is true, grandfather. He said he is not too old to be a father again," Milton told him.

"Ah, is his wife so young?" inquired Long King. Then he said sadly, "Some men are more fortunate than others. I have not thought lower than a woman's waist for many years."

After shaking his head a moment, he continued, "And Bean —how is the Indian commissioner? He is a good man."

"He is well, grandfather. He told me to give you his greetings if I should see you," Milton informed him.

The old chief motioned Milton off his horse. "Come, I talk too much while you wait. A malady of the aged, talk, talk, talk. We will smoke and we will talk a little while. But first, we will eat a little."

Eat. Always feed a visitor before you burdened him with questions and problems.

The old chief led Milton to an arbor covered by brush and bark from the many trees of the area. He walked to a split log stool and sat down. Long King motioned Milton to another stool.

A woman brought a bowl of lye bleached corn. Milton ate. It would have been impolite not to do so. Men of strength, of character, of worth, respected the customs of their fellow man.

Milton finished eating. A man brought forth a pipe with a clay bowl. This was not a ceremonial pipe, but a pipe to use when visitors came.

"Do you know Short Bow?" asked Long King.

"We have met," answered Milton.

Short Bow nodded a greeting.

"He is a novice religious man. He is keeper of pipes. The Spanish spirit men do not like our old ways or our religion. But it will not change as long as I live. If the people change after my body is gone and my spirit goes on to the other life, then that is their say," said Long King. There was no give in the old man's voice.

The novice "medicine man" was a man of mature years whose hair had begun to turn gray. A young man may be marked as a future leader in speaking with the spirits, but a young man was never given such a great responsibility or position. Men of youth could lead men into battle or they could lead a people as civil chief, but only men of mature years were learned enough to talk to the spirits.

Short Bow lit the tobacco with a live coal from a fire he carried in a clay pot and presented the sacred tobacco smoke to the four winds before he handed it to Long King.

Long King puffed the pipe, blowing the smoke to the four winds, then handed it to Milton. Milton performed the same ceremony. It was good, strong wild tobacco. The only kind the American Indian used. Only white men grew tobacco in cultivated fields like he did beans or corn. Tobacco was a money crop to the white man and had no religious value at all.

The same woman returned and left a bowl of cooked fish and a bowl of corn grits.

Three men joined them. They were Blanket, Gray Squirrel, and Poncho, all members of the council. They all acknowledged Milton's greetings.

Long King handed the pipe to Blanket, who performed the sacred ceremony of the pipe and passed it on. After the pipe ceremony, the pipe could be passed around for men to enjoy.

"Your fields are planted?" asked Milton.

"Yes. We think the last frost has passed. And our spirit talkers tell us that this will be a good year for crops," Long King told him.

"The *adawehi* of the Cherokees also say this will be a good year. Maybe not as good as last year, but a good year," Milton told them.

"Ah!" came from them all.

"The Cherokees are wise people and good farmers. It is well to listen to them when it comes to farming," said Long King.

The others agreed.

"Our head spirit-talker has been sequestered for days, trying to reach the meaning of a dream I have. I have had it many times," said Long King.

"What is the dream, grandfather?" Milton asked respectfully. As he had learned, dreams were nothing to be taken lightly.

"I dream that a black bird will fly down from the north. When he comes, trouble will follow. This black bird likes the red man, but he is driven away by white man. When he is gone, then the red man is driven out of Texas," Long King told him of the dream.

"All of the Indians are driven out?" asked Milton.

"I am not sure. It is not clear to me," the old man replied.

He took the pipe and puffed a few times. The rest of the men sat in respectful silence. None of them could make anything out of the dream. None of them would be so bold as to try and give an opinion. They did not have the power, and dreams were beyond them.

"White men keep coming in from the north?" asked Blanket.

"They come," agreed Milton to the question.

"Soon all Indians will be swimming in the ocean far to the west," growled Poncho.

Milton shrugged his shoulders. This was something he could do nothing about.

"The red man is a survivor. He can survive anything. Even the white man. Even the ocean," Long King assured them. Then he laughed in merriment. "A red man with gills and fins of a fish between his toes! That is indeed a thought!"

After the laughter died down, Long King looked directly at Milton. At that moment his old eyes took on the glint of his younger days. "So, you come after one of ours, eh, Tall One?"

"I do," admitted Milton.

"He is both feared and respected by his people. He is loved by few, hated by most, and respected by all. He is also trouble. I remember when he was a small boy. Just puppy size. He was always into some kind of mischief. As he got older, it changed from boyhood mischief to man-sized trouble. But still, he is Coushatta. A brave and fearless Coushatta warrior. A people needs its brave warriors," Long King told Milton.

The other men agreed.

Milton remained silent, waiting for them to have their say. He knew and they knew that even after they had had their say, he was still going to do what he thought he had to do. Nothing would change him. Nothing but death would stop him. All of them knew that.

"I have gone north with him to raid the Osage. He was the bravest of all," said Gray Squirrel. "We took many horses that the Osages had stolen from others. Some of these horses belonged to the Caddo. We gave the horses back to the Caddo. The Caddo people were happy to see their horses. The Caddo people have honored Thumping Turtle many times for things such as this."

"He was married to my sister once," said Blanket.

"He has been married to everyone's sister, once," laughed Poncho.

"That is true. Even some mothers have fallen to the spell of the big warrior," agreed Blanket.

"Why do you want to take him to white man's law?" asked Gray Squirrel.

"Because white man's law is the law of this country," Milton told him.

"Ah, no! We do not like their law. It is not good for us Indians. Why don't you just ride on out of here? You should not worry about their law," Poncho told Milton.

"I live in the white man's world. This is the white man's world," Milton said simply. He knew this would set them off, but truths are truths, no matter how it hurts.

"No! Not our world! This is our world! My world! This town is our world!" Poncho ejaculated.

Milton remained silent. Some men lived unlearned and they died unlearned.

"You breeds can come and go in either world and be happy. But I will never be happy in the white man's world. That is why I stay here, in our town!" Blanket barked.

Milton had to clear up some of these misconceptions before it got them all killed. "How long do you think the white man will let you stay in this world if they don't want you here? How many years does a red man keep a town? Before, in the old days my great-grandfather spoke of, a red man's town stayed in one place for hundreds of years. But that is not so in our time. Not in the day of the white man. So do not get too attached to your peach trees," Milton told them.

The three men growled. Long King remained silent.

The one thing Milton remembered about his great-grandfather was how he suffered because he had to leave his peach and orange trees behind. The trees now belonged to some white man in the old country of the Overhill Cherokees on the Little Tennessee River in what was now called the state of Tennessee. The old gentleman never forgot.

"You had better learn a fact. It is a wrong fact, but it is a fact. The whites, whether they be Anglo or Mexican, will get what they wish. If they wish land, then they will get land. And the white man always wants land. If he wants deer, he gets deer, no matter what the season. If he wants buffalo, then he gets buffalo, no matter if the calf's mother is killed to feed the white man's belly," Milton told them. He seared them with his eyes. "And if a white man wants an Indian, he will get an Indian."

"Not if we fight!" said Blanket.

"No! The white man will not have his own way. We will defy him. And his breed friends!" snapped Poncho.

Milton looked at him with neutral eyes. But the other men knew that their fellow tribesman had gone too far with this man. Poncho might well have to pay the consequences of his rash talk.

"I belong to no one. I speak for no one except Milton Hicks. I will not be put into any category by any man. Not even a Coushatta," Milton told them coldly.

No one made a comment, but they all understood.

"You say you will fight? That is a noble resolution, but not the responsible talk of the leaders you're known to be," Milton told them, softening his talk. He had been hard on them, but things would get harder before this country called Texas was settled. "At the present time there are more red men here in East Texas than there are white men, agreed? The red men could easily clear this area of all whites. But what then? The Mexicans would send an army that numbers in the thousands. The Americans could send even more. More whites would come to avenge those whites they never knew, just to kill red men."

He was kicking them in the stomach with his words. But it

was better to get kicked in the stomach with words than in the head with mule-hide boots.

"No, you dream a dream," he continued. "A dream that would turn into a nightmare for all of your people if you tried to force the white man on an issue. It is a dream. A noble one, but a dream nonetheless."

"He is right. He knows the score better than we who live here beside the river and seldom get farther than Prather's trading post," Long King admitted. "The white man is different than the red man. If a red man kills a white man, then he has hurt them all. If a white man kills a red man, then no one worries because he may have killed your traditional enemy. Those thoughts and alliances will defeat the red man."

"Some of the white men think well of the red man. Why do you think Bean sent me? Because he knows Piedras would willingly do Bean's job and come after Thumping Turtle. If Piedras came, he would come with two hundred of his soldiers. If he was successfully resisted, then he would come back a second time. The next time he came would be with an army large enough to destroy the town of the Coushatta and everyone in it," Milton told them, trying to convince them that they had to let some things pass.

"Tall One, we must know where you stand, is the reason I ask. If a war came, on which side will you stand, the red or the white?" Blanket dared ask.

"I am a survivor," Milton told them bluntly. "Our grandfather here said it, all red men are not truly brothers. Some of us are traditional enemies. I will survive as long as it does not get in the way of my honor. Then I will die in my honor."

In other words, I am telling you that I will not fight the white man on the side of an Osage, his mind told them, but he kept his peace.

Long King shifted himself on the stool and scooped a helping of corn grits into a bowl. Talking made him hungry.

"He is right, my sons. It is part of my dreams," Long King told them. "The white man will never let the red man rest until the Indian is controlled by the white man's rum and he has all of the red man's land. Then he will rub us all out."

Milton passed the pipe to Blanket. He told them, "It is not coming. It is here."

"But, Tall One, it is so very, very hard for a people to watch while one of their own is taken off to another people's justice," replied Long King.

Milton understood. He had seen it happen time and again. But this situation angered him. Thumping Turtle beat his own women and then had killed his white neighbor's woman while on one of his crazed drunks. A man such as he did not deserve such men as the great Long King to defend him. If the Coushatta had a law such as this of the Cherokee's, then they would have killed Thumping Turtle long ago for beating his women.

"At times you talk like a white man," snapped Poncho.

"I am part white," Milton informed him.

"Yes, Blanket, cannot you see? He is red on the outside and white on the inside," observed Blanket.

Milton started to rise, but Long King held up a hand.

"Hold! Hold, now!" Long King cried. He spoke to the men of his town. "I am ashamed of you. Is this the courtesy you will show when I am dead and gone? Is this the legacy I leave behind? A man has come and eaten of my food. He has smoked the pipe with us, sending the smoke of our sacred messenger, tobacco, up above. His smoke mingled with ours on this day. Does that mean nothing to you? Am I such a poor teacher and poor leader?"

The men sat, their heads hung as they were chastised by the elder. They were wrong. But, oh, it was so hard to keep silent at times.

The old man held the pipe in his hands. "Tall One, I ask you to forgive my 'young' ones. They violate every custom of our people. They think no more of harmony and tradition than the white man. Here, smoke with me."

Long King handed the pipe to Milton. Milton took four

puffs, blowing each in the direction of one of the four cardinal points. When he had finished, he handed the pipe back to Long King.

"The bond has been formed again, grandfather," Milton told the old man.

"Forgive us, grandfather. We acted as a young one with no mature years or experience," Blanket spoke for all three.

"Grandfather, this man has not only broken the white man's law, he has broken the law of manhood. He kills women. He beats women. If he is not stopped, he may someday kill one of my women. I will not allow this possibility," Milton informed the chief.

The old man sighed. Leadership of a man's people was much heavier as a man aged in years. "It will be a fight of honor when you two meet. I will demand it."

"I am a man of honor," Milton informed him stiffly.

"All right, Tall One. I know Thumping Turtle well. He will not go with you willingly. So, you will have your Cherokee vengeance. Or a try."

"That is all I ask," replied Milton.

"If you win, he will be dead and will not go to white man's justice. If he wins, you will be dead, and he will be forced to leave his people," Long King informed him. "So you will meet here. One of you will stay here."

The other three sat quietly.

Milton knew that Long King's conditions would prevail. Long King was the war chief, and in his position, he was responsible for the law and order of the tribe. He had control of the police force and the justice system. He would be obeyed!

These men were angry not because Thumping Turtle was going to have to answer for his crimes, but because the white man would be the one to meet out this justice and punishment.

"I will wait for him," Milton told them.

"He will be sent for," Long King informed Milton. "It will be a little while before he comes. He is going through the purification ceremony. He has drunk much of the white man's evil drink. He has been out among the white man."

Long King shuddered outwardly. He looked at Milton. "Wait here, Tall One. Be comfortable, my friend. You will be well fed and given drink. You are a guest of the Coushatta."

Milton thanked him for his hospitality by complimenting him on the good corn he had eaten. "I must care for my horse."

"One of the boys can do it," Gray Squirrel told him.

"No. This is a wild warhorse of the Comanche people. He must be taken care of by his master, who is now myself," Milton told them.

"Yes, their horses are as wild and uncivilized as the Comanche themselves," Long King told everyone. If he had time he would tell them about his encounter with the heathen Comanche years before.

They watched Milton walk to his horse, then lead it to water. While he was gone, the other men left to go about their business.

When Milton returned to the coolness of the covered arbor, fresh food had been placed at his disposal.

The sun was high overhead.

Chapter Twenty-two

There was a disturbance at the entrance to the village. A man and a woman rode into the town. The man was an Alabama Indian. The woman was a Quapaw.

Milton sat in the shade of the arbor, ignoring the young boys who had come to stare at him. They were brave. They were in their own village.

If the noise of the possible coming of his adversary bothered the tall man, it did not show outwardly. He was a warrior and had been committed to that station in life since his youth. The man already knew what all warriors know. Someday he would die in the violent terror of his chosen profession. The thought bothered him not. What better way for a warrior to die? Getting to be old with a shaky, feeble body, worn by age, to die at the feet of his great-grandchildren—soon a prospect scared Milton.

"You are lucky, tall man. You will have yet a little while to live," a boy of about twelve years told Milton. "When my father comes, your time will end."

The boy looked at Milton with unwavering black eyes. He was a proud boy. He would grow to be a proud man.

"What is your name, boy?" asked Milton.

"Mud Turtle," the young boy told him, standing a little straighter.

"You know this thing between your father and me has to do with warrior honor, don't you?" Milton asked the boy, not wanting a future enemy on his hands. This boy was innocent of things his father might have done.

"I know. Whoever wins or whoever loses, that's the way it

vill stand," Mud Turtle told him. His head lifted higher and
ιe said proudly, "You do not have to fear me, tall man. When I
»ecome a grown warrior, I will not come after you. I will not
»ecome a 'spirit chaser.' That is what you will become as of
oday. A spirit to seek its way to the afterlife."

"And if your father dies?" asked Milton bluntly.

"Ah!" spat Mud Turtle. Then he smiled. "It will not hap-
»en, white breed. But if he dies, you need not fear me. I will
ιonor the warrior's code. If you are so lucky as to kill my
ather, you will be safe from me. By the time I become a
;rown warrior, you will be an old man. It is no honor to kill
»ld men."

Milton smiled inwardly. The time of youth. Everyone over
hirty years of age was an old man. He glanced up from the
»oy to watch Long King as he came out of his lodge. The chief
vent to welcome the new arrivals. "Ah, welcome, Battise.
Iow are our cousins, the Alabama?"

"I don't know about the rest of the Alabama, but this one is
ιot and tired," Battise told Long King. Battise was wide of
;irth and not used to traveling such great distances as to
Prather's trading post.

"And the woman, Battise? Have you taken a new wife?"
ısked Long King with a smile.

"No, I am past the age of wanting a younger woman. An old
›ne will satisfy my hunger." Battise laughed at himself. Indi-
ιns were not bashful when it came to talking about nature and
ife's ways. "This is a Quapaw woman. I will bring her to my
own and have one of the young men take her to her people.
She was rescued from the outlaws in the Neutral Strip by
Milton Hicks. Is Tall One here? This woman would not pass
his town until she found out."

"Ah, would Battise pass his friend's town without stop-
»ing?" asked Long King.

"No, grandfather, I would not dare. But with a woman such
ıs this pushing a man, he will do a lot of things he wouldn't do

otherwise. And if I passed here without stopping to see you, I would hear about it for years to come," replied Battise.

"That you would. How is your old father?" asked Long King, ignoring Morning Light.

"He is well, even though he now has many, many seasons added to his life. He sends greetings," assured Battise.

"The son of a chief should give greetings for his father to his father's friends. And they are always well received by those friends," Long King told him.

"Milton? Milton Hicks, is he here?" Morning Light questioned the chief. She could contain herself no longer.

"Yes, woman, yes, he is here. I will direct you to him," Long King told her. He called for one of his granddaughters and instructed her to take Morning Light to Milton. He looked back to Battise. "And, you and I, my friend, can sit and visit."

"We live so close, yet we seldom see each other," Battise complained.

"A day's ride or two days' walk is not close at my age," Long King informed him.

Morning Light jumped from her horse and followed the Coushatta woman. The woman led her to the arbor where Milton sat, patiently waiting. She walked into the roofed area and stopped, looking at Milton with an expression that said she did not know what condition she would find him.

The Coushatta woman ran the children away from the arbor.

"I told you you were an old warrior," Mud Turtle scoffed at him. "A warrior would have to be past his prime to have such an old woman."

Morning Light jumped to her feet. "Get! Get from here before this old woman sends evil to bother you!"

The Coushatta woman did not ask who was in the right or wrong; she chased Mud Turtle off. The young do not defy the adult. At no time is there an excuse for such a thing. Unless, of

course, the adult is a war captive; that was different. A captive
has no rights except those he is given by the tribe.

Milton smiled at Morning Light. "Sit and eat."

A flicker of gladness flashed across her eyes when she saw
that he had come to no harm. Then it passed from her face.
She was a Quapaw and could not act as if she were as concerned as if he were a member of her own people. And with
her sickness, she doubted if she would ever feel free to think of
another man as her lover, let alone her husband. What if she
married another man or this tall warrior? What if he should
consider taking her as his woman? What if the union made a
baby? What would it be like? Eaten by disease even before
birth? But all of her problems would soon be ended, for she
knew the disease would not let her live much longer. Her
sorrow was her own. She would keep it.

She sat on another stool and helped herself to the food. She
asked him between bites, "Thumping Turtle is not here? Did
he run away?"

"He did not run away. He will not run. He is going through
purification," Milton informed her.

"Ha! That one can never become pure. Not even if the
headmen of his religion worked all their lives." Morning Light
laughed with no humor.

"You know him that well?" he raised his hairless eyebrows.

"Woman talk," she informed him.

"Oh?"

"At the trading post. And most woman talk is honest talk,"
she informed him haughtily.

Milton grinned. He liked women with pride and spirit. He
wished she did not have an such evil sickness. He would have
enjoyed a stay with her.

"Why must you take this Coushatta in to white man's justice?" she asked. "They don't treat a man of mixed blood as
well as they should. So why do you work for them?"

It kept coming from all sides. Only the strong could be a
breed in this world of solid colors. He knew how his friend

Will Goyens felt dealing with Anglos. Except that Milton was more lucky than Will. He could pass as white most of the time and was not bothered by the color line here in Mexico. Will had stuck himself in Nacogdoches with whites.

He had told her before, but he liked her. "I live in a white man's world. And even more important, if I did not take him back, the Mexican army would come after him. They would not care if it destroyed the town and everyone in it to take him back, dead or alive."

"Are you a better warrior than this man? Or is it a man's vanity that makes you think you are better?" She was blunt and to the point. She felt too much had passed between them for there to be any restrictions on her talk.

"It doesn't really matter one way or the other. I would still do what I had to do," he said, shrugging his shoulders.

"You have no fear, eh, great warrior?" she asked. He might not have fear, but she did.

He did not bother to answer that. It was not the idea of dying that bothered him, but the possibility of not being victorious.

"If the Coushatta man kills you, which of your people do I take you to for burial? The white people or the red people?" she asked tersely.

"Neither. You bury me here. Anywhere they will let you, is fine with me. Long King's people can say the proper prayers as well as anyone," he said. "That if is a big if, woman."

"Do you ever cry for your red people?" she asked, licking her fingers. When sex is not possible, a person might as well eat. Under other circumstances she would have demanded a place from viewing eyes for their last few moments together.

"Need I answer that?" he asked sharply.

"No," she said slowly, feeling that she might have shamed herself. "But we have so little time and I want to know you better."

She gazed off across the town for a short while, then looked at him. "If I had known you before my sickness, tall man, I think maybe I could have kept you in my village for a while."

She knew that no woman could hold this man for long.

"I think you just might have been able to do that," he agreed with a smile.

"Maybe we could have even made a baby," she said happily.

"Do you have children?" he asked. He had not thought to ask before.

"No. No more. I will die alone."

He had nothing to say to that. It happened too often.

"I had a baby girl. She was stolen by those bad Osage people. Then I had a little boy and another little girl. Then the white people came. They killed my little boy and my girl baby. They scalped my little babies while they were still alive. Then they took them by their little feet and bashed their heads against a tree." Morning Light sat remembering, pain on her face and in her voice. "They made me watch. And they laughed at my agony. Then our men came back from the hunt. The white men ran. One stabbed me here before he left."

She pulled up the blouse she had gotten at Prather's and showed him the wicked gash on the inner side of her left breast. Plug had cut the nipple off that breast. She was as scarred as any warrior he had seen, for there were other marks on her chest and stomach. He knew that they were the marks of an angry white man. She had been three years in hell as a captive in the Neutral Strip. Things would have been easier for her if she had not been determined to escape and had gone along. But she was not the type. He admired her.

Suddenly her conversation changed, as if she were determined to drive out the remembrance. "See, my new clothes? I have many more other things. That white man, Prather, he gave me these things. He told me the horses and all the things the outlaws left behind would pay for these things. I was given the horse we rode from the camp on. I carry the load behind me on the horse. He says I deserve these things. He is a good man, eh?"

"That he is," agreed Milton. "Kind of blows the idea that all white men are heathens, doesn't it?"

"Who to hate? Who to trust? It is enough to scramble the mind," Morning Light admitted.

Milton relaxed with his back against the post.

Morning Light looked at him. He was such a good man. Stern, but that was because he was a warrior. That sternness got in the way of the softer things in life, but it never got in the way of honor, duty, and concern for others.

"It is sad that little boys must grow up. So sad," sighed Morning Light.

"You would rather we remain little boys?" he asked her, not knowing what was running through her mind.

"No. No, that would be even more sad," she admitted.

"We can make some things into what we want. Most things we must accept as they are. That is the burden of life for some people. The Great One has made it that way, so why should we think on it?" he asked.

"Don't be so practical, tall man," she scolded him. "One must also dream, in day as well as night. The Great One also gave this to us. So, I will use it."

She was right, of course. But most dreamers had time to dream. A Warrior did not have time to dream of life and what it meant. Not a young warrior. Not if he wanted to become an old warrior. When he did become an old warrior, that was the time and place to dream and reflect on the philosophy of life.

"How many children have you fathered, tall man?" she asked with a smile.

There was no "if," but how many.

"I don't really know. But I am sure there are some. Maybe many." He smiled, remembering some of the possible mothers.

There were many good things in life for him to remember, if he took the time. Some of his best times were in his youth when he learned about the mysteries of woman. He mostly remembered the talks by the old men of the many wars they had been in. It seemed that every grown adult he knew had been to war. When he went to his grandfather's *asi*, a family sweat lodge, to hear the men talk, he heard story after story of war, glory, and honor. Death from war was talked about, but not much thought was given to it. Death came whether a man wanted it or not. Glory and honor came only to those who had enough strength to gain it. That was the true mark of a warrior. Some warriors were better than others; some were known only for their ability to be there when needed. He had decided from the first of his remembrance that he was going to be more than just a common warrior. He was going to be the best. The Creek Red Sticks and Jackson had given him that opportunity. Now at age thirty, he was at the beginning of his prime.

"Do you wish something to eat?" she asked.

"No."

"Something to drink?"

"No, I have had enough." He would keep his stomach free of burdensome food, because a warrior does not fight on a full stomach. He had eaten enough to add to the strength he would need.

They sat, relaxed, shaded from the heat of the early spring sun. Hummingbirds buzzed around a pot of water and honey that had been placed on a post for their benefit. The noise of children playing could be heard. A mother could be heard calling one of her children. A baby cried, and a dog barked—very domestic surroundings for a battle to the death to be brewing.

He looked at her with appreciation. They had taken a liking to each other quickly. They liked each other's company and each wanted to see that the other was well on his way to happier times. That was enough.

Chapter Twenty-three

The ripple of a commotion ran through the town and quickly circled it. There were shouts from different parts of the town that became a fountain of noise, rising into the air to fall indiscriminately about them.

Milton knew what the noise was about. He stood and picked up his knife and tomahawk, placing them in his waistbelt. He took his rifle and tied it to his saddle. This was a weapon that would not be needed.

"Is it time?" Morning Light asked the unnecessary question. There was no hopelessness in her voice.

Milton nodded his head. "Yes." He walked from the brush arbor, leaving her standing there, his huge pistol in her hands. She would put it away. He knew that when the combat started, she would be standing on the sidelines screaming her support for him. Woe to the person who questioned her support.

The people were gathering outside the town near the banks of the river. There was a cleared ground for religious ceremonies and dance. The area was also used for ball play and other games. The only other cleared grounds were the fields. He knew that they would not desecrate these grounds by shedding blood upon them in heated, personal combat.

Farther down the river was another area that had a parklike appearance. The grounds were cleared of all underbrush and the trees had been thinned many years ago by the Caddo. The Coushatta had kept it free of undergrowth.

Long King stood to one side with one other person. That man was the religious leader of the Coushatta. He was of mature years, but not yet old enough to be one of the ancients of the tribe. His face was painted different colors, his only clothing being a deerskin skirt around his waist and a headdress made of a deer's head. He wore the badge of his religious office around his neck.

"Tall One, you are a man of religion. We will respect your customs of talking with God," Long King informed Milton.

Thumping Turtle had not yet arrived. Milton knew that the Coushatta warrior would arrive in some dramatic manner.

The religious leader started the rituals of his people, asking the spirit helpers of God to be kind to their prayers and aid their fellow tribesman.

Milton stood a hesitant moment, not knowing exactly how to react. He had long been away from the teaching of the Cherokee, but he did still perform some of the old rituals. Like "going to water" and singing his war song before battle, if he had time. But he had long been among the white world. He did these things nowadays on his own.

He was not now in the white world. He walked to the river, took off his clothes, and walked into the water. He faced the east, dipping himself seven times under the water and chanting his war song.

When Milton returned to the clearing, Short Bull asked him, "Do you need war paint?"

"My white blood paints me," Milton said sharply. He was not sure about the need for war paint. He was a man in transition, carrying the religious beliefs of two strong peoples, which meant he was a man with constant internal conflicts.

Suddenly a fierce war cry came from the edge of the clearing. Thumping Turtle had arrived. He jumped from the tree line and into the clearing. He was painted from head to waist in his colors of war. His hair was plaited for battle and a black eagle feather hung from his right plait. His clothing consisted of a buckskin breechclout, the flaps painted with war designs, and moccasins. His only weapon was a French-made trade tomahawk. He had chosen his weapon.

He was as fierce looking as Milton had remembered him, a fine specimen of manhood. His people had not overstated his ability as a warrior. He was one of the best, which was all right with Milton. There was no glory in defeating an unknown warrior.

"You have come to fight the Great Warrior of the Coushatta, eh, breed man?" Thumping Turtle called across the fighting ground in a great voice. His presence alone would have frightened a lesser man.

"The Great Warrior of the Coushatta should not make his victory brag until he stands over the victim," replied Milton in an equally commanding voice. "I have fought many more battles than Thumping Turtle, yet here I stand."

Thumping Turtle laughed. "That is only because you have fought little boys, not warriors such as I. We, the people of the Coushatta and myself, will see how you fare on this day when you fight a true warrior."

"I will fare as always. Victoriously!" cried Milton. "And it will be an easy fight with a woman killer!"

"Aaaaaaeeeeeiiii!" cried an angry Thumping Turtle. "I will have your scalp, white breed! Then I will tan your scrotum for a child's rattle. You have now come face to face with the Great Warrior of the Coushatta. I will prevail. I have always prevailed!"

"If you fight as you brag, you will be a handful," admitted Milton. "But I have found that the braggart runs out of wind even before the fight begins. Then I butcher him like an old woman skinning a rabbit."

This was not a display of loudmouthed boasting. This was a custom of a people. A custom of the red man. A custom as important as the battle itself and its outcome. It was a custom that the white frontiersmen had adopted with a relish, most of them going to great lengths in trying to outbrag their peers in displays of bravado. Some of the white frontiersmen had bragged their way into state and national capitols.

"Get ready, white man. I will end your career as Indian

catcher for the white man. It will end here, this day," Thumping Turtle thundered.

Milton placed his belt and knife on the ground beside his leather shirt. Then he placed his floppy, broad-brimmed frontiersman's hat on top of them. He held his tomahawk in a huge hand.

The Coushatta people circled the fighting ground. These men were not fighting for the honor of their people. These two men were merely deciding which was going to impose his will on the other. No tribal council, no law or any group could prevent two men from a decision such as this.

Milton ignored the people around him. He knew that at this moment, none of them really liked him. Thumping Turtle might not be called "friend" by many of them, but it was Milton who was the interloper.

"White man, are you ready to feel the sharpness of a Coushatta warrior's blade?" called Thumping Turtle.

"If it is not dulled by chopping women's wood," returned Milton.

"I will shave your hair off in the fashion of the Cherokee to show you its sharpness. Then your ears will come off, along with your head!" cried Thumping Turtle.

"You brag too soon, Little Turtle," Milton told him.

"Little Turtle?" roared the Coushatta.

The two men closed. The fight was on.

Milton did not have time to see Morning Light's anxious face.

The two men charged into the center of the fighting area. Both men bent into a semicrouching position, their fighting stance. They stopped short of contact and glared at each other. They began to circle, looking for an opening.

"You get older, white man," said Thumping Turtle with a crooked smile.

"And you have gotten fatter since I saw you last," Milton informed him. He smiled, for he knew his next words would

anger his enemy greatly. "Fighting women doesn't keep a
warrior in shape."

Thumping Turtle growled in anger. He stood crouched
three inches shorter than Milton, but he outweighed the Cherokee breed by forty pounds. Thumping Turtle's light-brown
Spanish eyes smiled in anticipation. Conflict was also the nec-
tar of life for him. He expanded his broad chest and laughed.
"This man before you is all Coushatta warrior, skinny white
man. I have long ago denied my white blood."

They circled, both searching for an opening.

"Get the white dog!" came from the spectators.

"He is nothing but a white breed!"

"A Cherokee white breed!"

There was mocking laughter.

"If you can find his manhood, cut it off. My puppy is hungry!" a woman called.

There was much laughter at that.

Everyone knew that this duel was serious business. One of
these men was going to die today. But an Indian's ability to
laugh at all things, and see humor even in the worst of things,
has given him an edge in the scheme of survival.

Sometimes a fighter must make his own opening. Milton
feinted a strike. Thumping Turtle countered and the fight was
on. The clash of the two men was accompanied by a cheer
from the assembled people.

The time for bantering talk had ended. From this moment
on the two men would be serious. Dead serious.

Milton jerked his right arm free from Thumping Turtle's
grasp and jabbed the point of the tomahawk's blade into
Thumping Turtle's midsection. Milton had drawn first blood.
The wound was not crippling, but it made the Coushatta re-
lease his grip and jump back. Blood flowed freely from the
wound and spilled to the ground. Turtle made no notice of it.

The two men made swings and counterswings, sparring and
making moves of advantage. Only once did their weapons
make contact. Turtle tried a downward swing and Milton

blocked it. The tomahawk heads locked together and the men strained against each other with pure physical strength. Milton broke the lock by means of a swift left hook hurled with all the power he could muster. The blow knocked Turtle for a tumble. He quickly bounded to his feet and stood ready.

Milton looked at Turtle. The signal was given and the men charged, locking themselves together in a death grip. Turtle was heavier, but Milton stronger. One's weight counteracted the other's strength.

They stood locked a moment, each testing the other's strength. There was no need for a test of wills. This was a test of warrior expertise and brute strength. This was a fight to the death. Either would die before he would surrender to the other's will.

What Turtle lacked in brute strength, he had in stamina and endurance. He did not tire. Milton was also a man of strength and of extreme stamina and endurance, and he would not budge.

Both men recognized instantly that a grip such as they had could turn into a tug-of-war that could last for hours. Suddenly, as if by mutual arrangement, both men let go and backed off a pace. They circled like bulldogs, looking for an opening to strike.

They sprang at each other, clashed, and went down to tumble and roll on the ground. A tree truck stopped their roll and they parted. Both men jumped to their feet to circle and maneuver again.

The end was swift, as most tomahawk fights are. Thumping Turtle struck at Milton shoulder high. Milton used his left arm to parry the blow. A moment before Turtle's weapon struck Milton's left arm high up near the shoulder, Milton struck his adversary with a savage blow in the chest under his left arm.

Thumping Turtle staggered, still powerfully gripping the tomahawk lodged in Milton's shoulder. But his grip loosened and he fell to the ground. He knew that he would no longer need his weapon. He kept his eyes on Milton's face, defiance still showing bright. He lay clutching his left side.

Milton walked up to him and looked down.

A bubble formed from the blood in the left nostril of Thumping Turtle's nose. The bright sun was growing dim for him and he could just make out the tall man standing over him.

"Never," he gasped. It was a whispered defiance, but it was strong in its meaning.

Without hesitation Milton swung hard, hitting his adversary on the left side of the neck, as if he were chopping wood. The blade cut through veins, arteries, muscles, to the neck bone. The warrior was dead by the time the blade finished its travel.

A cry came from the crowd. It was a boy's cry.

Milton looked up from his handiwork and gave a sharp cry of victory. It was cut short as he sunk to his knees and then to the ground on his face. The stunning blow to his shoulder and loss of blood had taken its toll in a hurry. He knew that the blade of Thumping Turtle had reached the bone and broken it. He hoped that it had not destroyed the shoulder joint.

Morning Light was the last thing he saw.

Chapter Twenty-four

Morning Light had rushed to Milton's side, pushing and fighting her way through as people surged forward. Her champion was down and hurt. He needed her at his side.

She knelt beside him, gasping at the sight of his wound. She tugged on Thumping Turtle's tomahawk and pulled it loose, casting it to one side as if it was something vile.

"Water. Take me to the river," Milton managed to get out. The Cherokee thought of water as a sacred messenger to God and a purifier.

She motioned Battise to her. She told him, "Water. We must get him to water."

Then Morning Light barked orders to the people around them: "Stand aside. Everyone!" She held Milton's tomahawk in her hand.

The people looked at her, but no one moved.

Long King frowned with displeasure. "No Quapaw has any cause to order the Coushatta people to do anything. Be grateful, woman, that we suffer you to be among us. Only because Battise brought you and because Prather asked him to, do we refrain from casting you out of our town's gates."

"No, I will not stand quiet. My man here is a great warrior. Greater than any warrior present. He has the right to take a warrior's trophy. I will get it for him," she told them, moving toward Thumping Turtle with the sharp tomahawk.

"Wait!" cried Long King.

Morning Light was forced back to Milton's side by the push of the crowd.

"He cannot reach the afterlife if he does not have his scalp," a grandmother cried.

"Do you men who call yourselves warriors and you who are warriors' mothers wish to deny him that honor? Is that the way of the Coushatta?" she yelled with scorn in her voice.

Milton tugged at her skirt, but could not gain her attention.

"Well? This Quapaw woman is waiting," she demanded in anger.

Milton pulled at her skirt again. Morning Light reached down and patted his hand reassuringly.

Long King and the leaders huddled quickly. When the old war chief faced Morning Light, his expression was set and he showed no emotion. "If he demands it, it must be so."

"No," Milton got out.

Morning Light knelt beside him. "But your warrior's honor. It is your right!"

"It is a warrior's right, but I do not want it. What I think is right is important to me and my honor," Milton told her. "This man was not an enemy of war to me. His and my stars crossed and collided because of an outside force, white man's alcohol. Let it go. Let him rest in peace."

At that moment he had the Coushatta of Texas on his side. Murmurs of appreciation were heard from all.

There were many Indians who believed that if a man was scalped, then the man's spirit could not find the route beyond this life. Milton knew this was nonsense, or thought it was, but he respected others' beliefs.

"Battise, help this woman take this man to the river, my old friend. When he is able to travel, take him to your village where he will be safe," Long King ordered. "Not all men are honorable. Not even all of my own."

"I will do it," promised Battise.

"You have a strong woman, Tall One. She will be good for you. The two of you will make a strong baby. You will have good times together, you two. For as long as it lasts," laughed Long King. After many years of observing life he had noticed

hat it was hard for two strong-willed people to live in the
ame lodge for any length of time.

Morning Light and Battise helped Milton to the river. He
ay in the shallow pool they made for him, letting the purify-
ng water wash away the blood and the hurt.

The novice medicine man, Short Bow, came to the banks of
he river and built a fire. He placed a piece of steel in it and
fanned it to make the coals hotter. He brought the steel bar to
a white-hot condition.

Short Bow came to them. He urged them to take Milton
from the river.

They laid him on the grass, naked, on his right side, the ugly
wound of the tomahawk in full view.

"Hold to him tightly," he directed Morning Light and Battise. Then he bent close to Milton's ear. "I am going to cauter-
ize your wound. Be ready for the heat of the iron."

Milton knew what was coming. He had already placed himself in the state of a warrior.

When the hot iron was placed on the wound, he did not
flinch or move a muscle. He had now "set the pace of a warrior." Neither his breathing nor his heart increased under
stress, and he did not pass out from shock. They could cut his
head off and he would ignore the pain.

Morning Light moaned for him, nearly passing out from the
smell of the burning flesh.

When Short Bow had finished, he doctored and bandaged
Milton's wound. After many prayers he stood and told them,
"His wound is of flesh and muscle, with maybe a little bone
crack. It will heal. He will have use of his arm again. He needs
good care, which will help. That and my prayers."

"What do you mean by a little bone crack?" questioned the
suspicious Morning Light.

"There is no worry. I have used stiff bark to hold the bone
in place," Short Bow informed her. He will not be deformed."

"It is good," Milton told him, breathing steadily.

"If you say so, I will believe it," Morning Light told Milton. She knelt beside him to give him a drink of water.

Short Bow stood and waited. He was to be paid. The amount was not important. The act was. Only when the religious leader was paid for his services would his medicine work properly.

Morning Light went to where her horse was staked while he waited. She looked in her bags and took from it a piece of green cloth that she had gotten at Prather's. She returned to the river and gave it to Short Bow with the dignity that was his right.

Short Bow made no remark one way or the other about the worth of the cloth. But she noticed his eyes brighten when she handed it to him. If his medicine was any good at all, Milton would get the worth of it. Short Bow left, with promises that he would make sure Milton was able to ride before they left.

They found Milton's clothes and weapons piled neatly on the bank of the river nearby.

"We will go now," Milton told them.

"Wait. Wait until you are better," pleaded Morning Light.

"No. That will take days. If we do not go now, the fever will set in before morning. We will not be able to leave then. The Coushatta town will certainly have a burden if I stay. They will have to guard me and take care of our needs and wants. We will go today. Now," Milton ordered.

"The fever will come, from the wound, and still you wish to go?" demanded Morning Light.

"I have said it," Milton said tiredly.

"If it is a certainty that the fever will come, we should stay," Morning Light argued.

Battise did an important wise thing at that time. He stood to one side and kept his mouth shut. Battise of the Alabama Indians would not have advised anyone on anything at the moment.

"We will go now," Milton informed her again.

"If we go now, you may die on the trail," Morning Light said, a note of concern in her voice. She was frightened.

"Then so be it," Milton replied simply.

Morning Light stamped her foot. It would do no good to argue. She knew that they would go, now, this very minute. A person did not disagree or question a warrior's honor. Not that it was disgraceful to question him. It was because the decision had already been made before the man had started talking. The decision had been made when as a young boy he had decided that he would become a warrior. And the woman must either obey the man's desires or find another man.

She stood up, looked down at him a moment, and went to ready things. She could not help but have pride in her eyes, even though she was worried and frightened about what might happen.

Milton directed Battise to build a Plains Indian–style travois. They tied it to Milton's horse. The horse was not happy at all with that arrangement. He had seen other horses so disgracefully used, but he had never thought of such a thing happening to him. He was a stud, not a mare. He backed his ears and humped up his back, rolling his eyes. He was ready to break loose with a bucking display such as no one had ever seen before.

Morning Light calmly walked up to the head of the horse, looked him directly in the eye, and hit him squarely on the nose with a haymaker swing. The horse did not rear up. He stood still, shook his head, lowered his ears, and dropped a hip.

Milton smiled. The horse had met his match.

When the travois was ready, two men came over to assist Morning Light and Battise place Milton onto the travois. They tied him to the frame, and placed a doeskin blanket over him.

Morning Light got onto her horse and took the lead rope of Milton's horse. Battise would not go near the horse. The Alabama did not produce stupid people.

As they entered the trail that led out of the town, Long

King stood, arms folded. He raised a hand, signaling Morning Light to halt. The old war chief walked to Milton's side and looked down. "Tall One, the fight was fair. The fight was honorable, fought by honorable men. No one wishes to ban you from the town of the Coushatta. You are welcome as always. You are a friend to all of our people. You are welcome to come to our town anytime."

Without waiting for a reply he turned and walked off. He suddenly stopped and turned, "And you, Quapaw woman, any time you need a home, come to the Coushatta. A people can always use someone with strong blood in her veins."

The old man turned and walked to his lodge.

Tears came to Morning Light's eyes. Oh, if he only knew how bad her blood was, he would not want her at all.

"That old man," said Morning Light. "Life is supposed to be right and wrong, hate and love, enemy and friend. How can anyone dislike such as he?"

Milton smiled and drifted off into unconsciousness.

There were four more hours of light left in this day. Morning Light felt they would be far up the Trinity River by nightfall and that much closer to the town of the Alabama.

Battise followed on his horse. This was one time he was a follower, not a leader. He was happy with his position on this trip.

Chapter Twenty-five

Milton woke. Thoughts were dark in his mind. The world slowly brightened and the first thing he became aware of was that he was not on his way to join the Black Man in the west to guide him to the afterworld. He lay on a low cot in a small one-room log house. From his position he could tell that it was not the Mexican-style *jacal* with the logs standing upright. This building was of the southeastern–United States style with the logs lying parallel to the ground.

He knew before he looked around that he was in an Indian's house. There was no strong smell of stale, unwashed body odor or stale trappings of horse or mule. This house was clean and smelled of pine needles and sweet grass.

A young dog trotted into the house as if he belonged. He walked over to Milton and licked the man's face. After the lick, to show that he was in charge, he went to his water bowl and drank his fill. His thirst slaked, he moved back outside.

Milton smiled. He admired boldness and an I'm-in-charge attitude, even in an animal.

Remembering where he was and what had happened, he understood his condition. At the moment his shoulder did not hurt. He knew his first movement would change that.

He tried to get up, but couldn't make it. He fell back onto the small couch-style bed with a bang.

In a moment Morning Light was through the door and kneeling beside him. She looked concerned until she saw that his eyes were open and alive. Then she smiled.

"How long?" he croaked from his dry throat.

"You have wandered in the No Name Land for four days. It is good that you have found your way back," she told him.

"That long?" He had never been out that long before. He must have lost more blood than he'd thought.

She dipped a gourd dipper into a water jar. "Yes, you were that long on the trip. It could have been longer. I don't know how you survived the trip from the Coushatta town, but you did," she said, frowning to indicate how stupid she'd thought the whole enterprise. But she would not go into that.

He drank slowly and only a small amount. He knew that too much water, like too much food after a long abstinence, would cause cramps.

"We are in the town of the Alabama people," she informed him.

He nodded. He didn't feel like carrying on an extended conversation.

"Battise went to his father, the old chief, and asked that we be given a house. This one was empty. So, we are here," she told him.

He shook his head slowly, indicating that he wanted no more water. The fall had made his arm hurt. He hoped he hadn't opened his wound. If blood showed, Morning Light would throw a fit.

"You are now awake. You will eat. You will get well and be strong again. Strong enough to roam free," she told him. A faraway look came over her face and she told him, "A woman cannot roam free. I wish I could. I wish I could."

"You can roam with me. I think it would be good for a while. We would both enjoy the adventure," he assured her.

"It would be no good, tall man. At least, no good for me." She slowly placed the dipper back on the peg on the wall. It would be wonderful, but not practical. Someone always had to be practical, and the burden was on her.

"I would be good to you. I would travel slow. A woman's speed." He smiled at that, hoping that she would enjoy the humor, or that at least he could get a rise out of her.

"This I know, tall man, this I know. You would be very good to me. But it would not be good for me to roll up in a blanket next to you, knowing that I could do nothing. Lying there, night after night, feeling my blood rise in its passion, watching you bathe and still be untouchable. No, tall man, I will not die such a slow death," she informed him with finality.

"Maybe it will pass, this disease that eats off noses," he told her. He knew this was not the case. From the material he had read about this disease, it would end only with her death.

"No, tall man, I will live with my people until the time comes. Then I will go into the forest. I will not return," she said matter-of-factly. After a pause she smiled. "Ah, tall man, we could have made some strong babies."

She stood up and went outside. She sent a boy for Battise.

Milton could hear her moving about the cook fire. He was going to be fed whether he wanted it or not.

A short time later Battise arrived. He walked into the house and over to Milton. "Ah, Tall One has returned to us. I thought your life's spirit had left us and could not find its way back to us."

"I am here, Battise, I am here," said Milton. "Sit, Battise, and visit."

Battise eased himself to the floor and sat on a trade blanket that was folded for such use. Battise told him, "Sometimes the life's spirit goes far before it returns. I have been told of this."

Milton waited. He would hear a story, so he would not have to talk.

"When I was a young boy—this was back in the old country before we came here—one of our old men told a story. I will always remember it. It was about his life's spirit departing his body. This was in a war in which he was killed.

"This old man had been shot near his blood source by an arrow from a Cherokee bow. We used to be deadly enemies with the Cherokee in the old days. That was before we got smart and don't fight so much anymore." Battise grinned.

"But this old man was a member of a war party. He said his life's spirit left his body and traveled to the treetops, up over the field of battle. He saw the battle below. He saw his comrades come to his body. They, thinking that he was dead, left him as they ran. He saw a Cherokee come and scalp his head. He felt nothing. No pain, no fear, nothing."

Battise paused to share with Milton the food that Morning Light had brought in. She departed, leaving the men to tell their stories of war.

After filling his bowl Battise continued, "Then his life's spirit left this world and traveled fast, fast, through a dark place to where all his old friends and family members, who were long dead, had gone. He saw them all, yet afterward did not remember seeing their body forms. He talked to them all, yet no words were passed between them.

"Then a light, a bright light, yet of a soft, pleasing glow, appeared. This light told him that he was his guide. But the old man, who was a young man then, told his spirit guide that he wanted to return to his body world. He told his guide that he would like to stay a little longer on earth. He wanted to get more war titles and to become an eagle hunter. There was a beautiful woman he wanted to see again and gain more of her comfort. The spirit guide said he could return to this world for a while longer."

Battise took a drink of the corn gruel. He drank long, and belched in appreciation.

Milton's stomach didn't fare so well. It would take time.

"By the time he came back, his fellow warriors had returned to find his body. They pulled the arrow out of his chest and he returned to this life," Battise continued. "The men jumped back, afraid. But he assured them that it was he and not a ghost spirit.

"The arrow point remained behind, near his blood source. It was in his chest near his blood source for over fifty planting seasons. Then the spirit guide sent for him."

The story ended suddenly. This was not a story containing

a traditional religious or social message. It had no message at all. It was an interesting story to be told supporting the possibility of an afterlife. It was not known if this was God's intention after a man's death. Only a fool would try to determine what the doings of God were all about.

"Maybe it does tell us something. Perhaps it tells us that being scalped does not keep a person from going to the place above as God intended," replied Battise, happy with the thought. Some of his family members had been scalped and he would like to see them once again.

"Yes, that could be true," Milton agreed. He burped and made a face, the sour gruel burning his parched throat.

"His life's spirit would never have left this world if that were not so," replied Battise.

"Could be." Milton was not inclined to discuss a subject he knew nothing about. In fact, he never felt comfortable talking about anything concerning religion. He knew too little about it to speak of it and might offend God.

"I have thought of this story many times since I was a little boy. I have talked to some of the wise men of our people. We do not think that this is the same as a dream. This is different. We do not try to interpret this thing as if it were one. It is too big for such little men as we. None of us is big enough to understand it," Battise told Milton, yet he was talking more to himself than to his listener. "I think perhaps there will never be a man here on this earth to tell us what it means. The Spanish skirt-men, they say there was such a man, but I don't think this is so. If such a man existed, he would have explained these things to the red man long ago."

Battise sat a moment. He had told his story. Knowing that Milton was well, he got up and went off about his business.

Three days after Milton had returned to the world of the active living, Morning Light placed his breakfast beside him where he sat outside the lodge, soaking up the warmth of the morning sun. He liked to sit outside with his back against the building and watch the new sun fight its way through the thick foliage. It was a battle worth watching.

"You are on your own, tall warrior," she informed him bluntly.

He raised his hairless eyebrows.

"The old chief, the father of Battise, will send a man to guide me to my people. I will leave this place. I will go back to my people," she told him. She knelt and sat back on her heels, hands folded in her lap. They were rough, work-worn hands.

"You go, huh? You go and leave me to the mercy of these Alabama people?" He wanted to lighten the load of their parting.

"Ha! You will not have to call for mercy. Not from the looks of two of these Alabama women I have seen. The heat in their eyes is strong. The look on their faces tells all, and they would gladly fight over you in the town dance-ground. They can barely wait until I leave their town," Morning Light told him. "They make me sick, for I wish I were they."

"Ah, to hurry and get well," he said lightly.

"You will. They will see to that," she told him wistfully.

"And you up and leave me. It will be lonely with you gone," he told her honestly.

Brightness of that knowledge flashed in her eyes. After looking at him a moment, she said, "Oh, tall man, this is a sad day for me. But it is a day I knew would come."

"I knew it also. Stay awhile longer?" he asked, reaching for her hands.

She pulled her hands away, wiping her eyes with the back of one of them. "No I go. It is a blessing that I go. Now some other poor woman must take pity on you and feed you."

"When do you go?" he asked, knowing it was soon.

"I leave this morning. Soon. After I have fed you." She stood and looked down at him. "Ah, tall man, we could have made strong babies together. But life is life. A person must accept what the Great One has given him, or he must end his life himself if he is that unhappy. I will think on it."

Milton did not tell her not to talk of killing herself. He knew most red people would kill themselves rather than live disfigured or suffer a life of pain. He accepted it.

"Battise tells me that the agent Bean will be here soon," she informed him.

"Yes, a man came in last night with the news."

"I will go then," she told him, trying to keep from appearing distraught.

"When?" he asked again. He knew there was no delaying her.

"I go now. My things are ready. I can prolong this parting no longer," she said simply. She called the puppy to her, gathered her things, and walked off toward the horse pens.

"Morning Light, you are a beautiful, strong woman. I have missed something in my life by not having found you long ago," he called after her.

She laughed happily, and shook her bottom at him. She did not turn to show the tears in her eyes.

He would never see her again.

THE OLD-TIMERS

These two grizzled knights of the Old West never listen when folks say they're over the hill—they just use their true grit, their know-how, and a little luck to tame even the meanest young outlaws.

Look for The Old-Timers novels by popular Western author Jim Miller, in upcoming months.

☐ **THE OLD-TIMERS OF GUN SHY**
16565-2 $2.95

☐ **THE OLD-TIMERS IN THE SANGRE DE CRISTOS**   20032-6 $2.95